THE CALLING

THE CALLING

Cathryn Clinton

CANDLEWICK PRESS
CAMBRIDGE, MASSACHUSETTS

First paperback edition 2007

The Library of Congress has cataloged the hardcover edition as follows:
Clinton, Cathryn.
The calling/Cathryn Clinton. —1st ed.
p.   cm.
Summary: In 1962 in South Carolina, twelve-year-old Esta Lea is called into the ministry of Jesus and anointed with the gift of healing, but when her relatives decide to take her on a religious crusade she wonders if it is the right thing to do.
ISBN 978-0-7636-1387-7 (hardcover)
[1. Spiritual healing—Fiction. 2. Fundamentalism—Fiction.
3. South Carolina—Fiction.]   I. Title.
PZ7.C62883 Cal 2001
[Fic]—dc21   00-049370

ISBN 978-0-7636-3373-8 (paperback)

2 4 6 8 10 9 7 5 3 1

Printed in the United States of America

This book was typeset in Horley Old Style.

Candlewick Press
2067 Massachusetts Avenue
Cambridge, Massachusetts 02140

visit us at www.candlewick.com

This is dedicated to my parents, who've nurtured
The Calling in countless lives. With special thanks
to all those who have lived this story,
especially my brother, Richard.

Chapter One

The Calling

Not many wise men after the flesh,
not many mighty, not many noble, are called.
1 Corinthians 1:26

The calling came to me, Esther Leah Ridley, at the Jewels family reunion. "Esta Lea," I said to myself, "you are called of the Lord."

I was twelve years old. It was August in the year of our Lord, nineteen hundred and sixty-two. Don't you just love those words—"the year of our Lord"?

Sort of romantic and mysterious. I read them in a book and tucked them in my mind until my calling when I remembered them plain as day. I decided that those words would describe my life from then on. No doubt about it, my years were gonna be the Lord's, and I'd hope for the romantic and mysterious.

You may not understand how I got a sign from God at a family reunion, but in Beulah Land, South Carolina, where I come from, God, which also means church, and family matter the most. The two are always twined together like vines in a ditch.

You also got to understand our reunions. Food, talk, and beer make up some family reunions, but ours are full of pie competitions, ripe gossip, and long-winded preaching. We hold our reunions at the Beulah Land Healing and Holiness Church.

I heard that some folks play games and such at reunions, but the closest thing we have to a game is horseshoe pitching and outhouse tipping. And those two things aren't games; they are serious business, depending on where you are standing or sitting.

My sister, Sarah Louise, and I waited all year for the reunion. Finally the day was here. I woke up feeling poorly 'cause we had busted our guts with pies the day before. We got to eat all the pies that didn't meet my mama's taste bud tests. "Sarah Louise," I said, "I will never look another pie in the eye for as long as I live."

She groaned, rolled over, grabbed her stomach, and then covered her head with her pillow.

"Come on, y'all, get up. We got to get going. Y'all nearly slept the day away already." Mama's voice came up the stairs and slid under the door crack.

We went downstairs. Sarah Louise fed Baby Ben, and I fed Elijah, our dog. We didn't eat any breakfast ourselves.

"Here, y'all, help me load the food into the truck." Mama got up from the table too quicklike and lost her balance. She landed on the floor, and so did the peach pie that was in one hand and the coconut cream pie that was in the other.

Two leaps and one bark later, Elijah was at the pies. He licked those pies like it was his destiny. Some dogs are born hunters. They point with their noses and go rigid when they see a rabbit. Not our Elijah. No sir, he was a born licker. When he smelled a pie baking, his tongue shot straight out his mouth, and then he dropped down and rolled belly up, with his little paws a-flapping.

"All that's left is the pecan pie," Mama moaned. We all turned and stared at it sitting in the middle of the table. "I guess I'm only entering one contest this year: the pecan pie contest."

Things were not starting out too good, and I'd had such high hopes 'cause this was the day my daddy was asked to preach, and it was a great honor to stand in the pulpit of Jasper Abraham Jewels. My daddy would only get asked to preach once. He didn't fit two important preaching rules: he wasn't a regular preacher, and he didn't directly descend from the line of Jasper Abraham Jewels. Only the directly descended got to preach twice, and only the regular preachers spoke more than twice. My daddy is a Ridley. He just married into the Jewels family.

At one o'clock in the afternoon, folks started collecting at the church. They put the picnic tables end to end and covered them with red-checked vinyl tablecloths. Ladies piled the food on the tables. Then they stood around them, swatting flies off the food, gossiping, and watching the children. The children hollered and tormented one another, enjoying it tremendously. The men threw horseshoes, spat, and jawed. When it was time for the eating to begin, folks fell on the food, pushing great forkfuls into their mouths.

At last it was time for the pie competitions. Every woman in our family wanted to win a pie contest, so they entered quite a few pies, but usually my grandma's sister Opal won most of the contests. I think she swayed the pie judge, Uncle Bentley, who just happened to be my grandma's only living brother. He was an old bachelor with no sweetheart, but he always had a pie sitting on his kitchen table. Aunt Opal must have put them there. Uncle Bentley, being the kind soul that he was, didn't realize what he was up against. But I did.

Uncle Bentley ate through all the fruit and cream pie competitions first. Then, after sampling only two pecan pies, Uncle Bentley pushed back the bench from the picnic table, pulled his napkin out of his shirt, and declared, "I'm as full as a tick on a collie's behind. I can't eat one more bite. This here pie"—he pointed to the one in front of him—"is the grand champion." And wouldn't you know it, it was my mama's pie. The grand champion, blue-ribbon pecan pie.

It was a sign. A miracle. I shivered from my

bones out. This was our day. I knew it. Something special was going to happen.

Following the pie eating, we all settled into the church. There were about seventy-five people sticking to the wooden pews. Saved folks on one side, and unsaved on the other.

My daddy went up and sat on the platform. He was sweating like the outside of an ice-cold bottle of Coca-Cola on an August afternoon. He was wet through and through before he ever got into that pulpit. After looking at him, I prayed under my breath, "Do good, Daddy, do good, Daddy." Then I realized I was praying to my daddy and not to God. I changed my prayer to "Let my daddy do good, Big God. Let my daddy do good, Big God."

Daddy must have figured that since this was his one-and-only chance, he'd preach a sermon to raise the dead. He stared above the jet-black netted head of my grandmother's other sister, Pearl, and pointed out the window right behind her. I followed his large-knuckled direction and stared at those crooked and tumbled tombstones surrounding the church. Then I heard him yell, which was something he never did at home:

"The dead in Christ shall rise!"

"Amen, Brother!" came from the pews.

I closed my eyes and saw moldy old bodies covered with maggots lying in their coffins. Why, just the day before, Sarah Louise sang a song she learned at school when she was little: "The worms crawl in, the worms crawl out, in your stomach and out your mouth."

Not now, God, I thought, and stared out the window again. I didn't want to see no skulls and bony fingers pushing through the ground. Shuddering filled my body. Sarah Louise had to be seeing bony fingers too because she began to shake. I'll never know what Adele, my cousin who was sitting in the row behind us, thought, 'cause at that moment she farted.

I gasped and covered my mouth. If I looked at Sarah Louise, the laughing sickness would bust out of me. A loud whack boomed through the church as Aunt Phoebe Eileen, Adele's mother, fainted dead away. She did it to get everyone's eyes off her "angel baby." Why, Adele never did awful things, much less in public, much less in church. Or so her mama thought.

"I'm sure it's Phoebe's heart!" shouted Uncle Farley. He bent over his wife and started fanning.

"Get her some air! Get her some air!" Two other men rushed over, and between them they half carried, half lugged Aunt Phoebe Eileen out of the church. If you have manners, you say she's a big-boned woman. If you don't, you just say big woman.

I leaned over to Sarah Louise and said, "Sheer humiliation toppled that woman."

"That's the plain truth," Sarah Louise said, "and I don't lie in church."

My daddy didn't even blink an eye. I couldn't believe it. He kept on going, "And on that final Day of Judgment, on that great and awesome day of the Lord, when the trumpets sound..."

Sarah Louise leaned over, and her golden honeysuckle-smelling hair fell over her headband, nearly covering her face. She whispered in my ear, "That wasn't no trumpet."

We giggled for real until we heard my daddy say: "The whisperers"—his eyes bored a hole in my soul as he said that word—"I mean the gossips, and the liars, and the murderers, and the adulterers will be cut down and thrown into the fiery pit of hell!" His voice vibrated on the word "hell."

Ladies all around started fanning themselves with last week's bulletin folded up into little pleats. You could smell the brimstone and sulfur coming up from the pit, or was that one of my other cousins? Lucas and Virgil sat right in front of us.

"The sinners will be weeping and gnashing their teeth, and I tremble, yes sir, I tremble to think that one of you may be among them." Daddy lowered his voice a touch.

Virgil swallowed and opened his mouth right in Lucas's ear. He was belching in church on purpose! He looked up and saw Daddy staring at him.

"Don't think that you can hide your sin on that day. You can't lie to God. God will not be mocked. God will not be fooled."

Virgil turned back to Lucas, ran his tongue over his silver-covered front tooth several times, and whispered, "Bet you can't beat that one." Their mother whacked them both on the knees with a ruler she kept in her purse for that purpose.

My daddy's voice kept coming, rolling over me like waves. "Remember what happened to Ananias when he lied to the apostle Peter? He dropped dead. I can hear the apostle saying to Ananias's wife"—

and my daddy lowered his voice to a ghostly whisper—"Sapphira, dear, the men who carried out your husband's body are here for you, and they will carry you out too."

I was listening now. *Thump, bump, bump, bump, bump*—Aunt Opal slumped over. Was it the heat, the fumes, or the Holy Ghost? Her head kept bouncing on the back of the bench. Had to be the Holy Ghost. The men who carried out my Aunt Phoebe carried her out too. The sound of their feet beat a steady *bum, bum, bum* on the wood floor.

I sat there dumbfounded. I'd never seen my quiet, shy daddy like this. The Holy Ghost had taken him over. There was fire and wind in his voice. This was bigger than my daddy doing good.

I felt the air tighten around me. Everyone in the church sat stiff as yardsticks. You could see the tension by the pull of their backs and the tightening of their necks. My heart was kathumping.

"Those angel reapers sent by God to sift the wheat and the tares in that awesome Day of Judgment will not be fooled. I can see their sickles"—*whoosh, whoosh*—his hand cut back and forth across the platform as he dashed from side to side. "Sinner or saint, sinner or saint. They'll put us into two different piles: the sinners will be fit for the kindling of hell, and the saints ... ahh, the saints will be riding in God's heavenly chariots, air-conditioned limos, to their heavenly mansions on Gold Street."

Angel chauffeurs and giant limos? Sounded good to me.

He stopped to mop the sweat off his face with his handkerchief. His curly blond hair was a halo around his head, but his words were a halo of light around me. I was right with my daddy word for word.

And then I felt it. It was the yellow warning stillness in the summer sky right before the twister strikes, and then it was fifty million red ants biting me all at once. One day I would stand in a pulpit and preach with the wind of the spirit and the fire of God. God had called me. The calling that began with Jasper Abraham Jewels was in me. There was no doubt in my mind. It was special, holy, and inescapable.

The baptism of fire drenched my body in its fury, knocking me to my knees. I stretched upright with my arms toward God. "I hear ya calling me,

Lord," I said. Then I heard my daddy's words before he ever spoke them—God dropped them right inside my brain. It was a sure sign from God that I was called. I yelled them out right along with Daddy: "And so I ask you, where will you be? Roasting or riding?"

Chapter Two

The Anointing

But the anointing which ye have received
of him abideth in you.

1 John 2:27

The healing power came surging through my hand
ten months later. Shocked the tar out of me, it did.
My eighty-year-old grandma sat at our kitchen
table. "I just don't know what's wrong this time,
Brother!" Nana yelled. "I got such a pain in my
good ear, and that doctor won't give me any

medicine!" She was deaf in one ear and pretty near deaf in the other, and she always yelled. Maybe she thought that no one else could hear either.

My Uncle Bentley sat next to her at the table. Brother was Uncle Bentley's nickname, 'cause he was the baby brother, last of thirteen. He was only a few inches from her, but he yelled back, "Ruby Irene, we'll have a healing service this week just for you!"

That's when we heard it. A loud *thwack*, followed by a groan. Then a thud. Daddy pushed open the front door, and there was Peter Earl, my uncle, lying across the welcome mat with a permanent crease in his forehead. He had knocked himself right out.

"Drunk as a skunk," my daddy said as he dragged Peter Earl by the armpits through the front door and dumped him on the sofa.

Sarah Louise and I winked at each other, because that's what Peter Earl always did. He was our favorite uncle when he wasn't drunk, and sometimes when he was. He dressed slicker than a whistle and looked a little like Elvis.

When we were little, he'd taught us to shoot BB guns, and he'd taken us snake hunting in the creek behind our house. We'd killed copperheads and water moccasins with nothing but rocks. And then there was the time he took us for a ride in a girl-friend's convertible. He honked the horn all through town. The sheriff actually pulled us over, siren and all, and ticketed Peter Earl for disturbing the peace. Right in front of the courthouse.

"You know what this means, don't you?" Uncle Bentley said.

"Yeah," my mama said, as she stirred soup at the stove and balanced my bawling baby brother on her hip with her other arm. She prodded Elijah, our dog, with her foot. "It means he isn't working right now, and he must've been good and hungry some time in the last week."

"Or too drunk to see straight," my daddy said. "That's when he comes here."

Nana walked over and looked at the crease in Peter Earl's forehead. "Pity," she said, "he had such a nice forehead."

"It's a good thing I happened to be here," Uncle Bentley said. "It's another chance to set Peter Earl on the straight and narrow. He's gonna get saved someday."

"Back to your ear, Mama," my mother said to Nana.

"What's that?" Nana yelled. "You know I'm hard of hearing. Speak up, Glorybe!" My mama's name really isn't Glorybe, but when my Great-uncle Ray-Ray—who is dead and gone now, God rest his soul—first laid eyes on her red, round face surrounded by fiery curls, he said, "Glory be, that is the reddest baby I ever seen. Where did that baby get that red hair?"

It is still a mystery to this day, 'cause my nana never answered the question, but I think she knew that Glorybe was gonna stick, so she named Mama Gloriana Ray after the comment and the uncle.

"I'll pray for your ear right now," my mama said.

"Yes, yes, I need the touch of the Lord," Nana replied. "Will He look down from heaven and find me in my time of affliction?"

And that's when I saw it. A picture of Jesus appeared inside me. It wasn't a vision—more like a snapshot. I knew it was Jesus 'cause He looked like the man in the picture, the one that hangs on the wall of our Sunday school room at church. He had pearly skin, long brown hair parted in the middle, and soft eyes the color of strong coffee with lots of cream. He was dressed in a long white dress. A pale yellow light surrounded Him, and He was reaching out His hand and touching the man born blind. I'd heard Mama telling Baby Ben that story last night as I was putting on my nightie.

I walked over to my grandma and put my hand on her ear. "Right here, Jesus," I said. And a jolt shot through me, throwing me back. It felt like the time that I tried to unlock the electrical outlet with my mama's car key. A bang of lightning and thunder at the same time. I landed on my fanny, sucking hard for air.

"Esta, Esta Lea," my mama said, rushing over toward me. "Are you okay, baby? What got into you?"

I was still gasping when my nana said, "Why on earth are you yelling, Glorybe?"

My mama straightened up, almost dropping Baby Ben. Her mouth and eyes opened wide. She turned and looked at Nana. "I wasn't yelling—I was facing Esta Lea, speaking normal-like, and you heard me." She lowered her voice to a whisper and said, "What is my name, Mama?"

Baby Ben stopped howling. The room was still, so still I could hear my mama's breathing.

"Gloriana," my nana said in a quiet voice.

"Gloriana Ray," she said in a regular-sounding voice. "Gloriana Ray!" she yelled. Tears ran down her face. "The pain in my ear is gone, and I can hear. Thank you, Jesus! Hallelujah, I been healed!"

"Hallelujah," my mama whispered.

"Hot damn," Peter Earl said. He sat up from the sofa stone-cold sober and looked at me.

"I heard that, Peter Earl," my nana said. "I will have no swearing in my presence."

Uncle Bentley looked over at Nana and said, "Ruby Irene, listen here," 'cause Nana had started saying, "Hallelujah, glory to God. Hallelujah, glory to God."

Then Uncle Bentley boomed, "Ruby Irene, I'm speaking to you!" He paused for effect 'cause he was using his "thus sayeth the Lord" voice. He was a prophet of the Lord, and he was the preacher in our church. When he spoke in that prophet voice, even my nana listened.

"What, Brother?" Her little head swiveled around on her neck, and she looked him full in the face.

"I been wondering what the Lord has in mind for Esta Lea ever since the reunion. I knew He called her into ministry, but I wasn't sure what kind, so I sealed my lips, I did. Now I know. Ruby Irene, she's got it. I know it as sure as my name is Bentley Jewels. God has anointed her with a healing gift. Why, look at her! The Holy Ghost is all over that girl."

A solemn hush descended over the room, and all eyes were on me, sitting on my fanny, glowing with the Holy Ghost anointing.

"I think I just got saved," Peter Earl said.

Chapter Three

Asking

Ask, and it shall be given you.

Matthew 7:7

"Esta." I heard the whisper and looked around for Sky Shorts. Sky was my best friend. We were tighter than Aunt Phoebe's girdle.

"Where are you, Sky?"

"Here. Over here." I saw Sky peeking out behind the fountain that is smack-dab in the middle of the town square. The fountain never has worked, but it does have a big statue of Robert E. Lee in it. Lee's feet are turning a yellowish green color 'cause every twelve-year-old boy in town has to climb in the fountain and pee on Lee's feet without the sheriff catching him. It's a sign of manhood. That's what Peter Earl said, and he should have known. He did it thirteen times. He always was a showoff.

"Let's meet under the tank. That way I can see my daddy when he comes out of the courthouse," Sky said in a loud whisper. We both ran over to the World War II tank, crawled under the front of it, and sat in the shade. We had to hide from Hurley Shorts, Sky's daddy. He hated my family 'cause they "had religion."

"What's your daddy doing?" I asked.

"Arguing with somebody about school taxes. Says I ain't got a proper education, so he don't owe them a thing." Sky lived in a trailer outside of town. In the summer, we only saw each other when her daddy came to town, which wasn't too often.

Sky said, "I heard your nana got healed when you touched her. I can't believe it! Did it tingle or buzz or what?" Sky's face had a glowy look, like a light was on inside her, flickering through her skin.

"Yeah, she got healed all right. I saw a picture in my mind of Jesus healing someone, so I touched her. It wasn't a tingle or a buzz; it was a whoosh like I was a pool filled with healing water, and God pulled the plug. Healing just burst out. But why do you look that way, Sky? All glowy."

Sky's shimmering face got serious. " 'Cause this is my chance. I'm in the presence of holiness. You saw Jesus. Gosh, Esta Lea, you're like Joan of Arc. You're a living saint and you ain't even growed up yet." Sky wanted to be a saint when she grew up. Joan of Arc was her hero. She must have read the Joan of Arc book a hundred times. The school librarian kept it in her desk just for Sky. She read it every time her daddy was especially mean. As soon as she was old enough, she was running away to a convent to be a nun. Her mama was dead, and Sky figured that working for the church seemed like the best way to make a heavenly person proud. And besides, nuns married Jesus and that seemed a lot better than marrying someone like her daddy.

"Can I touch you?" With a timid look, Sky reached over to touch my arm. I jerked away.

"You ninny, it's just me, plain old Esta Lea. Look at my red hair, my bird legs, and the mole on my left arm. Here, look at my fingernails—they got dirt under them. Nothing much has changed in me. I ain't no saint."

"How do you know for sure? This may be my moment of destiny. I may get a vision. Maybe the clouds will roll back and the heavens will open. I'll see the heavenly army prepared for battle. Please, Esta, just touch my head and pray." Sky crawled out from under the tank and kneeled on the grass. She had her head down, and her hands cupped together, her palms lifted toward heaven. She wanted it so much, and I wanted it for her, so I crawled out and stood in front of her and touched her palm.

"Jesus, this is for Sky," I prayed, but nothing happened. The glow left Sky's face. She lay down on the grass with her arms under her head, staring up at the sky. I plopped on the ground beside her.

"I guess this ain't the time," Sky said.

My heart seized up at Sky's sadness. "I guess not," I replied.

"Well, all in God's good time, right, Esta? Ain't that one of your nana's favorite sayings?"

"Yep, she says it a lot," I answered. Sky had more believing in her than anyone I knew. She just kept a-hoping.

Sky stood up and said, "Even the shade is sweating under the tank, and it's too hot to lie here in the sun. Let's take our chances and walk over to the cannon."

"Yeah," I said. "I'm thirstier than a devil in Hades." The cannon, which was on the other side of the square, had a water fountain next to it. An old magnolia tree shaded both. We ran toward it, and Sky kept her eyes on the double doors of the courthouse as we ran. We each took a small swallow of the tepid water, and then took a second one to swish and spit. We dropped under the tree.

"I don't know why God didn't give this gift to you," I said. "I wasn't looking for it, and you've been wanting a vision or something for a long time."

We both sat there quiet for a while, and then Sky said, "I don't think my daddy is ready for me to have a vision."

I thought about what Hurley Shorts would do if he thought Sky was "getting religion," especially if she became a healer or something. "I think you're right. God knows this ain't a good time, so He's saving it up for later when your daddy don't matter. But why me, Sky?"

She thought for a while. "I think that God knows that you'll listen, like Joan of Arc. Maybe nobody in your church was listening for healing gifts anymore. God must've looked down and thought, 'Now what will surprise 'em and get their attention? Those folks in Alamain County need shaking up.' Then He laughed, winked at the angels, and said, 'I know, I'll give Esta Lea the healing gift.' So God said, 'Hey, Esta Lea, you with the red ears, are you listening? I got some healing to do. Get ready.'"

My ears blazed at the mention of their redness, and I pulled on the lobes. "Yeah, maybe you're right, but I thought healers were perfect, like God Himself. Or could act like they were, like Uncle Bentley does. That ain't me."

"That's for sure, Esta." Sky climbed up the back of the cannon and walked to the end and looked down at me. "This means that living saints or gen-u-ine"—she drew out the syllables of the word—"healers"—she pointed to me—"and I mean you, Sister, don't have to be perfect." She rolled her eyes upward and pointed toward the sky. "Only dead saints are perfect." It was a great imitation of Uncle Bentley.

"Amen, Sister," I said. Sky jumped off the cannon.

"Sky, Sky Shorts, where are you? Git over here!" called Sky's daddy.

I flattened myself and rolled under the cannon. Sky took off running toward the courthouse steps. When I heard a car door slam, I rolled out from under the cannon.

"Shoo-ey, that was a close one," I said to a crow that was sitting in the magnolia tree. I sat there hugging my knees close to my chest.

Maybe Sky was right about God using me as I was. Didn't seem to be any other answer.

Chapter Four

The Ordination

～

Ye have not chosen me, but I have chosen you,
and ordained you, that ye should go
and bring forth fruit.

John 15:16

The power of the Lord crackled the air like static.
Goose bumps shot up and down me, tickling the
hair on my arms and neck as I stood at the back of
the church. It was a week after Nana's healing. It
was revival meeting. I loved revivals 'cause people
got stirred up. You never knew what was gonna

happen when the Holy Ghost fell on people. Confessing, salvation, and signs and wonders could descend on the church.

We had arrived at church a tad late, which wasn't unusual. Morris Oaks, the head usher, marched us down to the front row. Church always fills from the back. Latecomers sit up front. I didn't mind. I could see better.

Morris nodded at Daddy and marched to the back of the church. Morris loved embarrassing my daddy, though he'd never say so. There was a twitch inside that man that I didn't trust, an inner fidget that didn't belong in church. He was as tall and straight as a telephone pole—and had about as much personality too.

Uncle Bentley walked to the front of the platform where the pulpit was and gripped the edges of it with his hands. "I'd like to welcome each and every one of you to our revival meeting. I'm believing the Lord-a is going to do great and mighty things tonight. The elders and I were a-fasting and praying all week." He turned and looked at Elder Wallace Suggs and Elder Floyd Wills, who were sitting behind him. Their red padded chairs looked like thrones. They nodded their heads in unison.

"That's right, Pastor Bentley," Elder Wallace said.

"I extend a special welcome to my nephew Peter Earl, who got saved last week." Uncle Bentley pointed to the rear of the church. Someone gasped. Everyone turned around and stared. There, coming in the door, was my Uncle Peter Earl.

"Glory!" Mama shouted.

"Hallelujah!" Daddy yelled.

"Thank ya, Jesus!" Nana shouted. Hand clapping and yelling filled the church.

"Come up here, Peter Earl," Uncle Bentley said. "I'd like you to give us a word of testimony."

The church quieted down a little as Peter Earl climbed the steps to the platform and took Uncle Bentley's place in the pulpit.

"The good Lord reached down from heaven, picked me up from the gutter —actually it was my sister's front porch—and put me inside her house. That very night I saw the healing power of the Lord. He anointed my niece Esta Lea. She touched my mama and healed her of deafness. It was a miracle." He paused to let those words sink in.

Silence fell on the pews. Blood rushed up my body. When it hit my face, I puffed out my cheeks and blew a gush of hot air out my mouth to keep it from busting out my ears. I was sure everybody already knew about the healing, but now they were all staring at me like they'd never seen me before.

"I decided right then and there that my days of sinning were over. I saw the light."

Uncle Bentley stepped over and put his arm around Peter Earl's shoulder and said, "Thank you for that word, Peter Earl." He turned to the congregation. "What a mighty change, Brothers and Sisters! Let's clap to the Lord-a!" He kicked his right foot and clapped his hands. Everyone joined in the clapping.

Then he turned to Peter Earl and said, "We know that you are destined for the ministry just like your granddaddy Jasper Abraham Jewels."

"Yes sir," Elder Wallace said.

"That's right," Elder Floyd chimed in.

Peter Earl in ministry? That would take some doing. On his better days Peter Earl was a salesman. He looked drop-dead handsome with his flashy clothes and eyes-half-closed Elvis look. He sold "specialty advertising" to the businesses in the small towns around Beulah Land. His company printed sayings on calendars, combs, and other little doodads. Why, Peter Earl knew every secretary, receptionist, and waitress in a three-county area and flirted with each one.

Sister Margaret pounded on the piano. Aunt Phoebe stood up and sang, "I saw the light, I saw the light. No more in darkness, no more in night."

People jumped to their feet, stomping and singing. What a start to the revival meeting! This was going to be good!

Willie Boyd, the captain of the football team, ran to the pulpit with tears rushing down his good-looking face. He looked out over the church. My breath caught in my throat, and I nearly choked as his eyes brushed mine. But then his eyes moved on to Sarah Louise. I'd liked Willie since I was ten, three whole years now, but he only had eyes for Sarah Louise.

She was staring back at him with shock-wide eyes. She didn't want him getting too much religion. He might settle down and run his daddy's hardware store on Main Street—by her way of thinking, he was her ticket out of Beulah Land.

Willie turned toward Uncle Bentley and looked down. "Here, Pastor Bentley, I can't take it no more! The devil has had his way with me." He pulled a packet of cigarettes from inside his black-and-gold letterman's jacket and threw them down in front of the first row of pews. His face was pale.

"Great day in the morning!" I said to Nana. "This looks real." And if it is, I thought, Sarah Louise would break up with him.

"Oh Lord," Sarah Louise whispered.

Uncle Bentley ran off the platform and over to the cigarettes. He jumped up and down on them. "I stomp you, Devil!"

I heard crying on the other side of the aisle, but I couldn't see who it was. The cries became loud groans. They were coming from the middle of the pews. I still couldn't see who it was.

"Stop staring, Esta Lea," my mama said in a loud whisper. "It ain't polite."

"Victory is in Jesus," Uncle Bentley said.

Aunt Phoebe sang, "O victory in Jesus, my Savior forever."

Uncle Bentley went back to the pulpit, wiped his sweat-shiny bald head, and said, "Who else will come to the altar? Who will join Peter Earl and Willie? The Lord-a is calling you. Get on down here!"

The groaning increased. I saw Morris Oaks

hustle over to the middle of the pews. His brother Billy was standing up by this time. Billy staggered down the aisle with Morris close behind him. Morris was whispering. When they got closer to me, I heard Morris say, "No, Billy! You can't! Shut your mouth, Billy!"

"Pastor," Billy gasped. He stumbled up onto the platform and doubled over. Something fell from his pocket. It was a deck of cards. Willie Boyd stared at the cards. His eyes bugged; then he blushed. My cousin Virgil ran up to the edge of the platform and looked at the cards.

"It's a naked lady!" he yelled before his mama reached him. She grabbed him by the collar as if he were six instead of twelve and weren't a foot taller than her.

"You just wait!" she hissed in a loud voice.

"Ow! Ow!" Virgil yelled as his mama pulled him back down the aisle.

Uncle Bentley bent down over Billy. "Do you feel the load lightening, Billy?"

"Yes, Pastor Bentley, I do," Billy answered.

Billy stood up straight. His acne-scarred face was calm. He swallowed hard and said in a solid voice, "I'm free, Pastor Bentley. I'm free. No more poker playing." He stared right at his brother Morris. "I'm through with gambling, Morris. I won't be going over to Clara's Diner in Pottsville with you anymore."

Head usher Morris Oaks was a gambler! Everyone looked stunned, but it didn't surprise me. I'd always known there was something about that man. But even I had a hard time believing what my own eyes saw next.

Morris ran up onto the platform, drew his arm back, and punched Billy square on the jaw. Down Billy went. He lay still. Morris drew his arm back again, turning toward Uncle Bentley as he did so, but Peter Earl grabbed Morris's right arm, and Willie grabbed his left.

"No you don't!" Daddy called from our pew, jumping up. Mama stopped him before he could run to help Willie and Peter Earl.

Morris shook his arms free, turned around, and stomped out of the church.

Billy Oaks didn't move. He was out, unconscious. Looked deader than a week-old, tipped-up beetle.

"We got to get him to the hospital!" Willie yelled.

Something jingled inside me. It was the same electrical jolt that I'd felt at Nana's healing. It was healing power! It took me a minute, but I finally put two and two together. If I'd laid my hand on Nana's ear and she was healed, maybe the same thing would happen to Billy.

I ran up to Billy. I laid my hand on his head and said, "Be healed."

Right away he opened his eyes and sat up. "Why, Esta Lea," he said, "what are you doing up here? What you got to repent of?"

Peter Earl started laughing and Willie joined in. Soon everyone in the church was laughing. All I could think of was that this healing anointing was no onetime thing. What was going to happen next?

"My Lord-a," Uncle Bentley said as he pulled his oversize handkerchief out of his pocket. He wiped the tears that were streaming down his face. "What a miracle You have given us tonight! Church"—he paused—"Church, listen up! We got to celebrate tonight.

"Come up here, Sarah Louise. Lead us in a song. Raise that glorious voice of yours up to the Lord-a. Let's fill this church with the praises of God!"

Sarah Louise went to the pulpit, flipped her hair back, scanned the congregation, and lifted her chin. "Would you be free from your burden of sin?" she sang. "There's power in the blood. Power in the blood." She made the most of the moment, singing like a country music star.

Mama danced down the aisle, with Baby Ben tugging on the hem of her dress. The ladies of the prayer circle followed. As I was watching them, my vision narrowed to a small tunnel of pink, and the voices around me grew quieter.

My legs slackened and I sat down on the platform. The tunnel grew, and I could see a man inside. He walked toward me; it was Jesus! He took my hand, and I went back through the misty tunnel with Him. We came out into a light-filled forest where a sawdust trail stretched out before us. Saints were on both sides of the trail. Jesus and I walked hand in hand until we came to a temple.

I wanted it to go on forever, but the scene faded and I rubbed my eyes. This was a walking, eyes-open movie. I wished Sky were here, so I could tell her. Uncle Bentley helped me up from the platform.

"What happened, Esta Lea? The look on your face was pure-t glory."

"I saw Jesus, Uncle Bentley."

"She's had a vision!" Uncle Bentley yelled. People started whispering. Uncle Bentley looked out at the congregation. "Quiet, quiet, Brothers and Sisters! The Lord has spoken."

He turned back to me. "Hold on to me, Esta Lea. You're trembling, honey. What else did you see?"

I sagged against him, to keep my knees from buckling. My voice came out wavery, like I was talking into a fan. "Jesus was surrounded by Bible folks. They looked like the pictures in Bible storybooks. Jesus took me by the hand, and we walked down a trail together."

"Did you hear that, church? The great cloud of witnesses is watching Esta Lea, and Jesus Hisself has called her into a ministry! Right here from our church!"

"We walked until we came to a temple."

"Do you hear that, Brothers and Sisters? The Lord-a is calling her to a path of greater glory! He is leading her into a healing ministry!"

Surprise shot through me. Jesus had given me a

healing gift, and pictures, and even visions. But a healing ministry like the preacher men who traveled all over? Me? Esta Lea? I didn't think I'd be ready anytime soon.

My mama was crying and Nana was saying, "Yes, Lord," over and over.

Uncle Bentley boomed in his prophet voice, "Lord-a, we see the calling and the anointing that You have on Esta Lea. Like Queen Esther before her, she has been called to save her people. Oh Lord-a, the people You will save, and the people You will heal!"

"Esta Lea," he went on, "kneel down. Right here. Right now." I looked up at Uncle Bentley. He was a man of God, so I knelt. He placed his hand on top of my head.

"Come over here, Elder Floyd. You too, Elder Wallace." They walked over and put their hands on top of Uncle Bentley's. I could smell the salt of sweat on their hands. "These are the words of Jesus," said Uncle Bentley. " 'Ye have not chosen me, but I have chosen you and ordained you, that ye should go and bring forth fruit.' Esta Lea, by the power of the Holy Spirit, in the eyes of the elders, and with this church as a witness, you are ordained."

"I can see it all," Peter Earl said. He stared above the congregation and cocked his head as if he were listening to something. Then he closed his eyes and said in a solemn voice, "The Lord-a is calling her to a healing ministry. We will travel from church to church, tent to tent, until all are healed. Then we will build a giant church. A white temple with a giant golden steeple, pointing to the Lord-a."

A little queasiness entered the pit of my stomach. Since when did Peter Earl say "Lord-a" like Uncle Bentley and the other preachers? And what did he mean about building a church? Who and with what money?

"I hear ya, Brother Peter," Sister Margaret yelled.

Loud *yes*'s and *amen*'s came from all over the church.

"Peter Earl," Uncle Bentley said, "you will go on a healing crusade with Esta Lea. You will leave next week. Sarah Louise will go along to sing. You will protect them from the wolves and the serpents—Satan's wiles. God saved you in the nick of time. For this first crusade, all the offerings will go for the overseas missionary work of the churches. Temple building is important work and should come after we've all had time to pray for more guidance."

I was called, anointed, and ordained. Next week I'd be sent out. I looked at Mama. She was crying and stroking Baby Ben's hair. He was sleeping, his head in her lap. I looked at Daddy and he was praying silently; his lips moved even though his eyes were closed. I looked at Sarah Louise, but she was looking at Willie. Only Nana was looking at me. She smiled and I smiled back.

And then I happened to see Peter Earl. He was staring at the offering plate. His right hand played with the change in his pocket. He saw my eyes on his hand, and he winked at me.

Chapter Five

The Timing

To every thing there is a season, and a time
to every purpose under the heaven.

Ecclesiastes 3:1

My great-granddaddy's cuckoo clock ticked in the
corner of our house. It struck twelve o'clock. When
the little bird came out, it opened its mouth and
whispered, "All in God's good time," instead of
"cuckoo." My breath caught. I couldn't move. Sky
floated in and pointed at the clock. I turned away
from the clock and bumped into Peter Earl.

His hair was flat on the right side of his head and stuck out on the left. Deep creases wrinkled his face, like he'd fallen asleep on top of a chenille bedspread. He pulled a gold pocket watch out of his pajama shirt pocket and stared at it. "There you are, honey. Time to get going. It's six o'clock."

Sky shook her head back and forth. Her long brown hair whipped around. It wasn't in a ponytail like it usually was.

"No, Peter Earl," I cried, "that's not the right time. It's twelve o'clock, not six. You aren't ready yet. Look at you." My stomach clutched my throat. I couldn't breathe.

I sat up from the dream. It was one of those humid nights that suffocated the air right out of you. I got up and walked downstairs. I cracked the ice cube tray, wiped my forehead with a piece of ice, then sucked on it, thinking about the dream. Something wasn't right about this healing crusade; I felt it deep down inside. Was it the timing of it? I went back to bed, and after a while I finally fell asleep.

In the morning I woke up with the cottony taste of fear in my mouth. It felt like a sock stuck in my throat. Last night's darkness sat on me, and I couldn't figure out what it was about.

"Time to get up," my mama called, and then I remembered the dream 'cause it was about time, the timing of God.

"Rise and shine and give God the glory, glory!" The song I'd heard my mama sing more than half the waking mornings of my life came up the stairs, ending with a loud "Rise and shine and give God the glory, glory, children of the Lord!"

"Esta Lea," my mama said at breakfast, "eat your grits and eggs."

I doused my grits with salt and pepper and then stopped. "Can't, Mama."

"Something bothering you, Esta Lea?"

I glanced at Sarah Louise. "Sarah Louise, get about your business," Mama said.

After Sarah Louise picked up her biscuit and left, I asked, "How do you know when it's the right time for something?"

"Hmm, Esta Lea, that's a good question. Let me think a minute." And Mama hummed some, which is what she usually does when she is thinking. "Remember Solomon in the Bible?"

"The one with a thousand wives?"

"That's the one," she said. "Well, he was also very wise."

"Had to be," I said, "to deal with all those wives."

Mama smiled. "I suppose so. Anyway, he said there's a special time for everything. A time to be born, and a time to die; a time to laugh, and a time to cry; a time to keep silent, and a time to speak. Everything has a time."

"I know that, Mama, but what is God's timing?"

"All these things are in God's timing, Esta Lea. Ain't no part of life that's outside God's loving eye."

"But then, how do you know when God is saying 'Right now'?" I asked.

"He says it in all kinds of ways."

"You mean like through fiery preaching, miracles, and healings?"

"Well, sometimes in those things. But mostly I feel His peace, and I listen to that still, small voice in my knower."

"How do you know it's God in your knower?"

"Getting to know God is like getting to know anybody, Esta Lea. You spend time with them, listening and watching, and pretty soon you know what they mean."

"I guess I got a lot to learn, Mama."

"We all do, sweetie pie. Now get over to your nana's. It's your day to help her."

Nana was singing in the backyard, so I went around there. She straightened up from the garden and pushed at the small of her back with her fists. "Hey, honey," she said, and then pointed to a basket of laundry that was sitting on the back porch. I started pinning up the clothes.

"Nana, do you really think Peter Earl got saved?"

"Sure do. Don't this new round clothesline just beat all? Now that I have more room, I can plant more garden."

I liked the old line better. It went from her back porch out to the shed. It was on a pulley, and you could yank it in. I loved yanking. "It's something all right," I said, "but do you think Peter Earl's ready to be a minister and go on a healing crusade right away?"

"Why, Esta Lea, my daddy changed overnight when he got saved! Now finish hanging up those clothes. Then it will be time for a cookie break." She went into the house.

I went back to the laundry. I decided to tell

Nana about my dream. She was a great believer in dreams and had the gift of interpretation. People came from all over to get her say-so on dreams.

"Nana," I called, banging the screen door. "Nana, I got a dream to tell you." She hurried downstairs, her few curls bouncing around her head. She was tilted forward as if her tiny feet couldn't keep up with her.

"Well, let's hear it, Esta Lea."

I told her the dream. Nana nodded and smiled. "Why, that is simple," she said. "The clock is the calling of God that began with Jasper Abraham Jewels. It's in your house because it's your calling too. Peter Earl has a clock, or a pocket watch, because he's called too. This is God's timing for you and Peter Earl."

"And what about Sky?"

"Sky stands for all the people who need healing."

I wasn't sure about that. Sky needed healing when it came to her daddy, but she wasn't sick or crippled, and she knew more about God than I did. It seemed to me like she'd been warning me when she shook her head in the dream.

"What about the difference between the clock and the watch, and why a gold watch?"

"The different time means get ready, and gold is for the heavenly streets. It's a heavenly message you'll be bringing," said Nana. She put a plate of cookies on the table and turned around and busied herself at the sink.

I shifted from foot to foot, and then scraped my toe along a crack in the linoleum. It still seemed like something wasn't right. I wondered if this was my knower speaking to me, the one Mama talked about. Who was right? Esta Lea, a girl, or Nana, who was old, with lots of God-hearing years?

I grabbed two cookies and let each bite melt into my tongue. Uncle Bentley would say that we must be careful about questioning "God's anointed who labor over us," and Nana was one of God's anointed ones. But Peter Earl's itchy hand in the church service kept bothering me. I had the same tickle you get when a flea jumps on you and starts crawling around. You can't see it, and you sure can't catch it, but you know something's wrong 'cause it bites the dickens out of you.

"Esta Lea, since you're done with chores, could you get my prescription for me?" Nana's hearing was better, but her high blood pressure wasn't.

"Sure," I said. I could study the makeup in the

magazines at the pharmacy. I wasn't allowed to wear any makeup until high school, but I'd be ready.

Then as I was walking to the pharmacy, it came to me: I could talk to Patsy Ann Slocum about Peter Earl.

Chapter Six

Sure Election

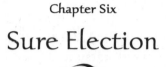

Give diligence to make your calling and
election sure: for if ye do these things,
ye shall never fall.

2 Peter 1:10

The door banged open as I walked into Slocum's.
"Hey, Esta Lea," called Patsy. "Grab that door, will
ya, and push it hard. It's broke again. How you
doing, honey? You're big news in town."

"I'm okay, Patsy." Patsy Ann Slocum was Peter
Earl's off-again, on-again girlfriend. Had been for

the last twelve years or so. They officially started going together on her sixteenth birthday, when she was homecoming queen and he was her escort. Everybody thought they'd get married, but they didn't.

Her daddy shuffled toward me, and I quick reached out toward Patsy and handed her Nana's prescription before her daddy could take it from me. Everybody knew that Patsy filled the prescriptions. Her daddy couldn't remember much anymore.

"Papa," she said, "why don't you go back to stacking the vitamins. That job needs to get done." He went to the other counter and placed one vitamin C bottle on top of another.

I put a dime and ten pieces of Bazooka Joe bubble gum on the counter and said, "Patsy Ann, I got a question for you."

The door opened. It was Aunt Phoebe Eileen. I knew her by the sound of her breathing, a small gasp followed by a snort. I ducked and snuck to the back of the store where the magazines were before she could see me. If she heard my question, everybody in town would, and this was too private. About fifteen minutes later, after a long conversation with Patsy about heart medication, Aunt Phoebe left.

"You still back there, Esta Lea?"

"Yeah," I answered. "I'm looking at the makeup." Someday I'd buy that cornflower blue Maybelline eye shadow. The pink pearl blusher and eyeliner sent a deep longing into my heart too. Tearing myself away, I walked to the front of the store and stood near Patsy. "Do you really think Peter Earl got saved? I figure you know him better than most."

She pulled on her earring. "Well now, Esta Lea. You know I don't take to that church business. I ain't been in one since my mama died when I was thirteen, but it's obvious that church does take for some. Why, look at your mama and daddy." She paused. "But Peter Earl, he's a horse of a different color. It'll take more Holy Ghost power than I heard of to knock the devil out of that man. Wait and see is my motto when it comes to Peter Earl. If he keeps his hands out of the till and off the bottle for more than a few weeks, I might believe God Almighty is holding tight to them. The proof is in the pudding, baby."

"Nana believes he's saved and changed."

"Your nana believes the best of people. She always looks for some good in 'em, and, honey, I appreciate that. She's almost persuaded me there's something to this believing business." She started laughing and said, "Why, she probably says that Morris Oaks will be back in church next Sunday."

"You must've seen something good in Peter Earl, Patsy."

"You're right about that, Esta Lea. I seen parts of him that nobody else has. Like the night my mama died." She turned and stared out the window, and her voice softened.

"Nobody thought twice about me. They were crying over my mama's dead body and hugging my daddy's hands. I was hiding. You know where the pines come together in a tight bunch around the brick barbecue? If you duck through the viny stuff and pull apart the barbed-wire fence, you can crawl through. On the other side, you're in a place with a carpet of pine needles and a snug roof of branches. That was my thinking place." She leaned on the counter and sucked in a deep breath.

"Don't stop," I said.

"That night when your gramma's family came over, Peter Earl came looking for me. He was sixteen. He called my name, but I didn't answer. I was willing him to find me. It took him a long time, but he did. He never said a word. Held me while I cried.

He didn't tell me everything was gonna be all right, or she was in a better place, or it was all for the good. Finally I fell asleep. When you go through something that hard, you get a tight place down inside you, Esta Lea. If you share that tight place with someone else, especially when you are a kid, you don't ever forget that person. There's something between you that's deeper than hell. Mind you, Esta Lea, nobody else knows this. It's our little secret."

"Cross my heart and hope to die," I said.

We both crossed our hearts, and then Patsy went on. "When you love somebody, you got to see them for what they can be. But"—she paused and looked me right in the eye—"you also got to see them for what they are. Can you picture the mountains in North Carolina, Esta? The ones up 'around Asheville?" I closed my eyes and nodded.

"Well, Mount Pisgah is what Peter Earl is, and Granddaddy Mountain is what he could be. In between the two is a deadly drop. So far I ain't seen no way across."

I opened my eyes. "But Peter Earl saw a miracle, Patsy." My voice trembled.

"I believe ya, honey. There's no denying miracles. It's the everyday living that kills ya."

One tear slid down my face. My question about Peter Earl had settled down into sadness. Patsy Ann had doubts about Peter Earl's changing and so did I, but it didn't matter 'cause Peter Earl, Sarah Louise, and I were leaving at the end of the week for our first healing meeting.

It felt like two giant hands were pushing my shoulders down, bunching the muscles in my neck. Must be the weight of glory that Uncle Bentley was always talking about. I picked up a Slinky that was sitting on the counter and walked it from one hand to the other.

"Any more questions, Esta Lea?"

I bit the inside of my cheek. "What about this healing crusade with Peter Earl? How could this be the right timing?"

"Don't know much about right timing, but don't worry, hon. This trip may not turn out to be all you think, but I can promise you one thing: It will be a good time. Always is with Peter Earl. Besides, he'll take good care of you. He always did before, didn't he?"

"Well, yeah," I said. It was true. Peter Earl had lived with us many a time, usually when he was in a tight spot with money. He loved us, no matter what else he did. I knew he'd watch me with a good eye; I was just afraid his other eye might be watching God's money.

"Besides, Peter Earl's a cat," Patsy Ann said. "He always lands feet-down when he falls."

The front door opened, and two old ladies came in. They were the oldest sisters in town, Mrs. Wheatly and Miss Pruitt. They did everything together. As the sisters walked toward Patsy, she handed me Nana's prescription.

"Be seeing ya, hon," Patsy said. Then she smiled at the two sisters and said, "Hey, Mrs. Wheatly, Miz Pruitt. How you two doing today?"

I headed toward the back door. Mr. Slocum was ahead of me. He opened the door and followed me out. I turned him around and lightly pushed him back inside the store. "Thanks, Patsy Ann," I called, and pulled the door tight.

Chapter Seven

Preparations

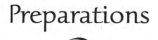

Prepare ye the way of the Lord.

Isaiah 40:3

It was the weekend, and in about an hour we were to leave for the Lukewarm No More Church in Chancellor. Chancellor was a couple of towns away, right on the county line. It was our first meeting in the healing crusade. I was jumpier than a cricket in a bait bucket. Healers probably pray some to get ready for their services, I thought, but I couldn't think of anything special to say, so I prayed two words, "Help, Lord." I said them until they sounded funny. I wished that Sky were going with us. She could come up with all sorts of words when it came to talking to God. Then my mind drifted to Peter Earl and his "preparations," as he called them.

He was already in Chancellor getting ready. "Show people what's coming and then make them wait," he said. "It lets them know how important you are." I knew I wasn't the important one because Jesus was the healer, not me, but I didn't know what Peter Earl thought about himself.

This led me to further prayer. I just changed the words from my earlier prayer from "Help, Lord," to "Lord, help."

Peter Earl's plan was that first Sarah Louise would sing to get hearts inspired, feet tapping, and hands clapping. Then he would follow with his own word of testimony, which would stir the folks. After this, when people were in a state of "religious expectation," as Uncle Bentley called it during revival services, I would pray for healing of the sick.

A horn tooted out front. Through the chintz

curtains of my bedroom window, I saw Peter Earl in a golden convertible Cadillac with big tail fins. It looked like his boss's. I ran outside.

"Peter Earl, is this your boss's car? How did you get it?"

"Well, now, my boss knows that I am a sober sinner, and he jumped at the chance to help in the Lord's work." Peter Earl winked. "For one night, that is. To get things started right."

"It's Peter Earl," I called back to Sarah Louise.

She ran outside and jumped in the back seat of the Cadillac. "I feel like the Queen of Sheba in her chariot. This is destiny. I sense it. I will meet my King Solomon."

"I hope he doesn't have 999 other wives, like the real one. I declare, Sarah Louise, can you keep your mind on the Lord, and off of Solomon? Besides, what happened to Willie Boyd?" I asked.

"I've come to my senses. Willie Boyd is Sticksville. Willie Boyd is the town of my birth. Willie Boyd is football, and proms, and his daddy's hardware store on Main Street. I am putting away childish things, Esta Lea. Why, I am destined for greater things. Mark my word."

Nana rushed out, followed by Mama. Nana had

come over to see us off. She looked at us and cried, "I give you up to the work of the Lord."

Peter Earl grinned at me.

"They're only going to Chancellor," said Mama, "and I'll be over there for the meeting."

"I know, but it is Esta Lea's first healing crusade, and we're the ones sending them off."

Mama handed us two scarves, saying, "To keep your hair from blowing. I don't want all last night's pin-curling to be ruined. Y'all look so pretty." We had on our best dresses. Mine was the color of ripe cantaloupe, and Sarah Louise's was a shimmery blue. Mama blew a kiss and said, "God bless. I'll see y'all shortly."

Daddy came outside, wiping his hands with a towel. He'd just come off a swing shift at the Celanese material factory where he worked. Baby Ben was tugging on his pant leg.

"You take good care of my girls, Peter Earl, or you got me to deal with. Don't forget the eye of the Lord is upon you." Daddy picked up Baby Ben and kissed us each on the cheek. Baby Ben leaned over and licked us both.

"Pretty is as pretty does!" Nana yelled as we drove away.

We picked up Route 442 and headed toward Chancellor. Sarah Louise had that still look that meant her mind was elsewhere. Probably in a land of cream and honey and Solomons aplenty.

We rolled into Chancellor in grand style. It's a town a lot like Beulah Land. Folks sit on their front porches for entertainment. Nothing like your neighbor's life for some good laughs.

We passed the Pins-a-Plenty Bowling Alley. Orange, purple, and marigold-yellow papers were stapled up on the telephone poles along the street.

"Look!" I yelled to Sarah Louise. "Must be a big-top circus coming to town. Think we can go?" She didn't answer. Saving her voice for the church singing, I supposed. We drove by McCullum's Variety Store and the post office with its wilted American flag. Looked as thirsty as I felt. Then we pulled up in front of June's Café.

Peter Earl walked in and we followed him. "Hey, Dora," he said to a woman who walked with petite high-heeled steps that caused her rear end to rock and her polyester skirt to ride up. Enough to notice. And Peter Earl did, until he caught my eyes on him.

I had an idea that Dora might be the main reason that Peter Earl had come to Chancellor before he picked us up. Some preparations!

"Long time no see," Dora said with a giggle.

"Girls," Peter Earl proclaimed, "this is Dora, June's daughter," like we were supposed to know who June was. When we didn't say anything, he added, "June of June's Café."

"Oh, sure," I said. "Pleased to meet you."

"Y'all are here for the big show, or so Peter Earl tells me," said Dora.

" 'The big show'?" I said.

"Let me see. I believe the flyer says 'The Lord's healing, howling, hopping hour, starring Esta Lea.' "

" 'Howling'?" Sarah Louise and I said at the same time. We both stared at Peter Earl.

Dora rubbed her temple, almost upsetting the carnation perched on her ear. I could see this effort at thought was costing her a lot. She said, "Let me see. Oh yeah, 'The deaf hear, the blind see, and sinners confess. Must see and hear to believe. Come on down and get your free gift.' "

" 'Free gift'?" Sarah Louise said.

"The picture must be you." Dora stared at me. "Though you don't look much like it."

"What picture?" I asked Peter Earl.

"Hmm, it must've been the last school picture your mama gave me," Peter Earl said.

"Peter Earl, I don't think Mama's given you a school picture since I was in second grade. I had a scab that covered my nose and a disgusting frizzy perm that Mama gave me."

"Pretty is as pretty does," Sarah Louise said.

"Hush up!" I told her.

"Y'all sit down, and I'll bring ya some food," Dora said.

We settled into silence. Dora put plates of fried chicken, mashed potatoes, gravy, and snap beans in front of us. "Where did you see this picture?" I asked Dora.

"Outside on the telephone pole. Actually, they are all over town. They look like circus posters."

Sarah Louise and I jumped up from the table and ran outside to the nearest telephone pole. There I was on a marigold flyer. My face was scrunched between the words "healing, howling, hopping," and "deaf, blind, sinner." The picture was mashed up somehow, like the mimeograph had a crinkle in it. I looked like a dog with a perm, a cross between Little Orphan Annie and Sandy, her dog. I started crying, but Sarah Louise giggled.

"She walks, she talks, she crawls on her belly. It's Joe-Joe the dog-faced girl." Sarah Louise busted up and sat down on the sidewalk, she was laughing so hard.

Joe-Joe the dog-faced boy was our favorite side-show at the carnival. He was better than the bearded lady, the two-headed calf, and the man with tattoos on 90 percent of his body.

"What's this howling I hear?" Peter Earl said as he came outside.

"Joe-Joe the dog-faced girl is warming up for tonight," Sarah Louise managed to say between laughs. She stood up and said, "And so am I." She hopped from foot to foot, howled, and then yelled, "I'm healed, I'm healed!"

How could she make fun of me and my calling? On the first day of our crusade! The sight of her laughing face cooked my blood to the boiling point. I wanted to shake that howling right out of her. I grabbed for her shoulder, but she stepped back so fast, she turned her ankle and fell to the sidewalk. I heard a ripping sound and knew that her shimmery blue dress was torn somewhere.

"Look what you've done, Esta Lea!" Sarah Louise shouted. "My very best dress!"

"Oh Lord," Peter Earl said. "Stand up, Sarah Louise, and let me see the damage." She stood up and turned around slowly. There was a long rip right down the back of her dress. "You are going to be more work than I thought. You two still fight like dogs. Esta Lea the bulldog versus Sarah Louise the yappy Chihuahua."

By this time, Dora was outside too. I guess she heard just the end of the conversation because she said, "I have a dog."

"Don't tell me," I said. "It's a poodle."

"How'd you guess?" Dora asked.

"Holy Ghost power," I said.

"Wow!" Dora said. "Psychic!"

Peter Earl groaned. "Esta Lea, that does it! Go over to the church. Just look for the steeple. It's only two blocks away. Stay there until it is time for the service."

He turned to Dora. "Do you have something Sarah Louise can wear?"

"Sure. And I'll get you a cute little hat too," she said to Sarah Louise. "Spruce you up a bit. I always wear something on my head. Flowers when I'm working, hats when I ain't."

This time Sarah Louise groaned.

Maybe Chancellor was prepared for the Lord's meetings, but I wasn't. I stomped to the church. I didn't have a healing thought in my head.

Chapter Eight

Healing

The blind see, the lame walk, the lepers are
cleansed, the deaf hear, the dead are raised,
to the poor the gospel is preached.

Luke 7:22

Peter Earl wasn't a dummy. He knew that sending
me to the church would work on my heart. Nothing
like a silent church to quiet you and turn your
thoughts toward God. I stared up at the pulpit and
knew there was no way I could stand up there as
unworthy as I was. Guilt was oozing out every
which a way.

Just then I heard a chattering noise. It drifted in the window by the first pew. Must have been a squirrel. It reminded me that I better get back to chattering myself.

"Lord," I prayed out loud, "I don't see how You can do one thing tonight here in the Lukewarm No More Church. I am a lousy rotten sinner and I know it. I must be the sorriest excuse for a healer You've ever seen."

I wandered downstairs to the Sunday school rooms in the basement. The familiar church basement smells of wet carpet and tuna casserole from last week's fellowship meal greeted me. I pushed open the door to one of the classrooms, wandered in, and picked up the paper they sent home each week with the kids. There on the front page was one of my favorite stories—Balaam and the donkey. Balaam was a bad prophet who wouldn't listen to God, so God told a donkey to speak to him. Balaam listened to the talking donkey. When God does something unusual like talking through donkeys, it makes you sit up and take notice.

I picked up the paper, wandered back upstairs, and sat on the first pew. The words "If I can speak through a donkey, I can speak through you" popped into my mind. It had to be God because I couldn't come up with something that good. *Sky was right. You don't have to be perfect.*

"Okay, God," I said, breathing a tremendous sigh of relief. "I ain't much better than a donkey, but if You still want to use me, I'm willing." I heard the chattering sound coming in the window again. It sounded louder than a squirrel. What was it?

"God," I silently prayed, "I appreciate your speaking to me, but it would be helpful if You also gave a sign that You wanted to use me. Something like an animal speaking your words."

Nothing happened, so I got up and walked to the window. The chattering noise was coming from the house next door. There in the backyard was a monkey with a collar around his neck. A chain went from the collar to a long wire that stretched across the backyard. The monkey ran back and forth along the wire. Sometimes it turned flips.

People were entering the church. A small, round man with a fleshy jaw line and wire waves for hair marched up front and pumped my hand. His whole body, including his jowls, jiggled as he pumped my hand.

"I'm Pastor Dennis, and you must be Esta Lea. Hallelujah. I'm so pleased as punch, yes I am, to have you here at the Lukewarm No More Church. Praise God. We heard the good things the Lord was doing in your church, hallelujah, and we just knew we had to be a part of it...."

My, I thought, this must be why God sent a donkey like me here. This man was not going to let God get a word in any other way. He was talking a hundred miles an hour.

"We've been a-praying for revival, for the out-pouring of the Holy Ghost, hallelujah, for signs and wonders, and we just know that God is hearing our prayers."

He was still pumping my hand with all his might when Sarah Louise walked in. If she hadn't been my sister, I wouldn't have recognized her. She had on a yellow suit with white gloves. A small white hat sat on top of her hair, which was pulled up into a twist. She looked a good two or three years older.

Sarah Louise turned to speak to Dora, who walked in beside her. From Sarah Louise's chatty nod and smile, I saw that she and Dora were becoming friends. I couldn't believe it! How could Sarah Louise betray Patsy Ann? Patsy Ann was supposed to be Peter Earl's girlfriend, not Dora!

Dora wiggled her fingers at me, but I just stared at her. Wiggling must be her main means of movement, I thought. Feet, rear end, fingers, head, the woman was a walking wiggle. Even the leopard skin, Hershey's Kiss–shaped hat on her head gave a jiggle.

"And you must be Sarah Louise, hallelujah!" Pastor Dennis dropped my hand and grabbed for Sarah Louise's. "I heard the Lord has given you a golden voice, praise Jesus, the voice of an angel." Sarah Louise pinked up and looked down at her toes.

I skipped up to the front pew and sat down. Sarah Louise slid in beside me.

"I'm sorry about your dress, but it doesn't seem that losing it hurt you too much," I said.

"Actually, Dora has given me this outfit, so I thank you for ripping that old blue thing. No forgiveness needed," she replied coolly.

"Where is Peter Earl?" I asked. The church was about half full, and I was getting a little worried.

"I don't know. He just dropped me off and said he'd be back later."

A family came down the center aisle and sat right beside us. The daddy was dressed in overalls and a buttoned-up white shirt, and so was his son. "Much obliged to ya," the daddy said as we all wedged in closer. "My name is Winford Samples, and this is my son Ezra. The rest of the family is down there." He turned to the little boy beside him and spoke in sign language.

"Well, I declare," Sarah Louise whispered to me, "that is a little deaf boy on our row."

"I know, I know," I told her. I prayed silently, "A totally deaf boy—that's more deafness than Nana, Lord, but You are the healer; I am not." And then I added my all-purpose prayer "Help, Lord," to cover anything else.

I turned to look for Peter Earl and heard him yelling outside, "Come and get it! Get your free gift!"

People were flooding into the church, filling up the seats. Peter Earl ran to the front and jumped up on the platform.

"What is he doing?" I asked Sarah Louise. "We don't have any free gift."

"I know, but remember the posters all over town?"

"What's the free gift?" a red-faced man called out.

"You'll have to wait and see," Peter Earl said.

Pastor Dennis went up to the platform. "I'd like to welcome each and every one of you here tonight. Hallelujah. It's good to see you, Mrs. Sawyer, praise God, and you too, Mrs. Rays, oh, and the Springs family. I'm so glad to see you." I groaned. This could go on forever, but Peter Earl jumped in.

"Yes, well, thank you, Pastor Dennis. I was wondering if you could introduce my nieces and me."

"Oh yes, this is Peter Earl Jewels, and his nieces Sarah Louise and Esta Lea Ridley. Praise God. The Lord has called them into a healing ministry, and we have the pleasure of being the very first church in their healing campaign. Thank you, Jesus. Come on up here, girls."

We joined Peter Earl and Pastor Dennis up on the platform and sat on the benches there. It was scary to have the eyes of the church on us. There was a knock on the door, and then it opened.

A girl about my age was resting her arm on top of her mother's. The girl wore a pink flowered dress, and she had soft-looking, nearly black hair. She walked up the aisle with a slight shuffle, staring straight ahead. Her mother was leading her. I realized that the girl was blind. Behind them walked a young boy, a man, and another woman. Her family, I supposed. The only sound in the church was the tapping of their feet on the wooden floor and the congregation's quick intakes of breath. The family came up front and sat down next to Dora.

My heart jumped up and pounded my ears until I couldn't hear anything else. "Oh God, oh God, oh God, help! A deaf boy and a blind girl!" I whispered. I looked down at my feet. I began to sweat and my palms itched. Sarah Louise went to the pulpit to lead the hymn singing. I sat there, unable to open my mouth when everyone else sang.

I stared at my Bible sitting next to me on the bench, and I saw the Sunday school paper sticking out of it. *Yes, the donkey. The donkey and Balaam. Thank you, Jesus. You are the healer.* God was the healer. I was just the donkey. My heart slowed and a huge space opened around me. This wasn't up to me. My ears opened and I could hear Sarah Louise singing her special number, "Faith, mighty faith, the promise sees and looks to God alone. Laughs at impossibilities, and shouts it shall be done."

I hummed along.

Pastor Dennis left the platform and walked down between the pews. He said, "Let's all stand up and join in."

Everyone did. "And shouts it shall, it shall be done, and shouts it shall, it shall be done. Laughs at impossibilities, and shouts it shall be done." And then they began to sing in tongues. Everyone but me. I'd spent a lot of tarrying time at the altar, waiting for the gift of a prayer language, but I still didn't have one.

Tongues is the heavenly prayer language that the Holy Ghost gives to folks. You give up praying normal words, and the Holy Ghost prays heavenly words through you. I do believe that some folks just use it as a filler during long prayer meetings. Sometimes God gives a special message to someone who speaks it out in tongues. Then another person interprets God's message. To be honest, I'm not always sure that the interpretations are from God, because they can sound like someone's two cents' worth. But every now and then, you get a good announcement.

Everyone was singing in tongues with their eyes closed and their hands raised. I turned my palms up and stared out the window by the first pew. And then the little monkey climbed in. How had he gotten loose? He scooted along the floor and sat in the front row where no one else was sitting and folded his little hands like he was praying. I looked over to Sarah Louise, who was standing beside me. She saw him too and struggled not to giggle. The monkey yammered away, and, I swear, I couldn't tell the monkey's voice from the heavenly tongues. It blended right in.

Soon everyone stopped singing except for the monkey. He kept yammering. Since the congregation was standing with their eyes closed, no one but Peter Earl, Sarah Louise, and I could see him. Sarah Louise was actually holding her hands over her mouth to keep her giggles in. Finally the monkey stopped and a woman at the very back stood up and gave an "interpretation."

"Yes, you are unworthy, but because of the blood of the Lamb you are worthy. I send you forth to do my work. Go in the name of Jesus!" She spoke in the general way that these prophecies can come, but I knew it was straight from God to me 'cause it was exactly the words I needed to hear!

Then after a long pause the woman added, "I am calling from the trees, 'Let my people go!'"

Somehow I didn't think God was saying that part. That was either the woman giving her two cents' worth or monkey ESP. Laughter bubbled out of Sarah Louise and me like water spilling over the dam at the reservoir. We couldn't stop. My ribs ached from laughing.

Peter Earl drew himself up tall and said, "Thank you, Sister, for sharing that word. While you folks are still standing, reach into those pockets and purses for your money. This special offering will go to the overseas missionary work of your church."

The ushers came forward to take the offering and started passing the plates. Sarah Louise and I finally got quiet. I remembered my prayer, "Lord, let an animal speak," and I was sure that God had heard it. There was no doubt in my mind that He was going to do something wonderful tonight. Faith filled me up, puffing me from the inside out.

The monkey sat there good as gold during the offering. They brought the plates back up to the front of the church and handed them to Peter Earl, who bowed his head and prayed, "Lord, we thank You for this offering. I mean for blessing us, so that we can bless You." At that moment the monkey jumped up, grabbed an offering plate, and ran out the window. "Damnation, you furball!" Peter Earl swore, and ran out the side door after him.

We started laughing again, and this time Dora joined in. I heard a sound somewhere between a laugh and a choke and looked out to see Mama stand up with her hands over her mouth. She ran out the back of the church. I guess Peter Earl and the monkey were too much for her too.

Poor Pastor Dennis didn't know what to do. He ran his hand through his wiry hair so many times that it stood straight up. "I think we better skip Peter Earl's testimony," I said to Pastor Dennis between gasps.

"What about the free gift?" the red-faced man called out again.

"Sarah Louise, can you give us another song?" Pastor Dennis said. Sweat was rolling down his face.

Sarah Louise went up front and sang, " 'Tis so sweet to trust in Jesus, just to take Him at His word, just to rest upon His promise, just to know, thus saith the Lord."

I felt the sweetness of Jesus flood me. Complete

peace. I knew that He would work through me, for He had given me a sign. I closed my eyes, and I saw the picture of Jesus healing the blind man.

"Okay, Lord, this is Yours, not mine. You do it," I prayed silently. I walked down off the platform and leaned over the first two pews and asked the blind girl if she wanted me to pray for her.

"Yes," she answered.

Her mother led her up to the altar railing. "Holy Spirit," I said, "we ask You to come and heal this girl, as Jesus healed the blind man when He was on the earth. We know You are the healer."

We waited for two minutes in complete silence. Let me tell you something: Two minutes is a long, long time when the unbelieving eyes of the church are on you. Then the girl screamed and fell to the floor. She kept screaming and Dora began screaming too. Oh no! I thought. What have I done? Sarah Louise rushed down beside me.

"Hush up!" Sarah Louise said to Dora. Sarah Louise and I picked the girl up.

"Look at me," I said to the girl. I took both her hands in mine.

"I can't," she answered. "It hurts. What is this bright pain?"

"It's the light!" her mother yelled. "She's never seen the light!" The church hushed, frozen in astonishment. The only sound was the soft crying of the girl's aunt and Dora, who kept saying, "Oh my Lord," as she crossed herself. She must have been Catholic in some other life.

The girl held my hands and opened her eyes. They were creamy white, with no pupils, but as I watched, pupils began forming. The girl's father sobbed as she turned and said, "Daddy, Daddy, is that you?" She put her hands on his face, touched it, and said, "It is you, Daddy." She turned to her mother, her aunt, and her brother and touched them, placing the touch with the face. She stared at them as if she couldn't get enough and was afraid to close her eyes.

People were crying all over the church. Pastor Dennis knelt on the floor and said, "We are in a holy place."

I hugged the girl and asked, "What is your name?"

"Althea, Althea Reynolds."

"I'll never forget you, Althea Reynolds."

"Nor I you, Esta Lea."

"Thank you, Jesus. Thank you, Esta Lea," her

mama said between sobs as she flattened my hands between hers.

Peter Earl came in the back door and looked around. The offering plates in his hand were empty. This didn't look good. He couldn't have given the offering to the pastor or deacons 'cause they were all in the church. The offering was probably in his pocket. Then he saw Althea Reynolds. He grabbed for a pew and sat down, dropping the offering plates.

No one helped Althea as she walked out the back doors of the church. People filed after her with a peculiar quiet. Even the red-faced man forgot to ask what the free gift was. I agreed with Pastor Dennis—we were in a holy place. I turned to pray for the deaf boy. I placed my hands over his ears and prayed, but nothing happened.

His daddy looked at me and said, "Don't worry, we ain't giving up." I thought that man had mountains of faith.

It was obvious that Peter Earl hadn't believed anything was gonna happen in church that night, even though he'd seen Nana's and Billy Oaks's healings. Neither had Sarah Louise or Pastor Dennis, or anyone else in the church except maybe Dora.

Somehow I didn't think that believing in things was a problem for Dora—she probably believed in aliens. But nobody else thought that healing would come for all their talk of faith. The shock was too widespread.

I skipped out of the church and twirled in circles on the grass. Finally, I got so dizzy I sat down. "Thank you, God!" I shouted at the top of my lungs.

God had taught me a lesson. One I hoped I wouldn't forget. He used donkeys, monkeys, and Esta Lea Ridley. I didn't have to be perfect, only willing. I couldn't wait to tell Sky about this. Believing that God could use me had taken more faith than praying for Althea Reynolds's healing.

Chapter Nine

Pondering

~

His mother kept all these sayings in her heart.
Luke 2:51

The next afternoon I was dusting the end tables in the living room and listening in on the conversation on the front porch. Sarah Louise and Willie didn't know I was there 'cause the curtain was drawn across the open window. Sarah Louise had just taken two glasses of ice tea outside, so I figured she was warming up to the best part of her story.

"Esta Lea," Mama called.

I ran into the kitchen and said, "Hush, Mama, you got to hear this!" I motioned for her to follow me. We sat on the sofa right under the window. Sarah Louise was talking.

"And, Willie, I knew that God wanted that poor blind girl to receive her sight, so I stood up and sang, 'There's power in the blood.' Then I pointed at her and said, 'Rise up and be healed,' and she stood up healed." Both Mama and I started laughing. Sarah Louise jumped off the porch swing and stomped into the living room. She was madder than a yellow jacket caught between the door and the screen. "Were y'all listening to my private conversation?"

"Yes, we were," Mama said.

"No, Mama, that ain't quite right," I said, and giggled. "We were listening to Sarah Louise's tall tales."

"Sarah Louise, you ought to be ashamed of yourself!" Mama said. "That is fibbing, plain and simple. I worry about you! Your mind is filled with nonsense and dreams of glory. What will be the good of it? Are you trusting God at all?"

Sarah Louise dipped her head and let her hair fall across her face. Actually her hair is in her face a good deal of the time, 'cause she is covering up what is written across it.

"I trust God a little and myself the most," she told us. "Now I know I could trust God more and I will someday, but right now my dreams are gonna take me out of Alamain County and on to better things. As to the story, I might have gotten a little carried away, I admit."

"A little?" I said, and yelled out the window, "Willie, if you want to hear the true version of the story, talk to the monkey that lives next to the Lukewarm No More Church. The monkey was faithful to speak God's truth."

Sarah Louise's face was screwed up tight. She was fit to be tied! "Esta Lea, if Willie weren't here, I'd pop you so good. You don't understand me. But I understand you. You have been waiting for your moment of glory. People always took notice of my singing, but not of you. And now they do." Then she pointed her finger at me and shook it. "I watched the look on your face, Esta Lea—the red-pleasure look that filled your face when the little blind girl got healed. You loved being the center of attention."

I covered my ears with my hands and squinched my eyes shut. I didn't want to hear any more!

She whirled and ran from the room. About a minute later I heard Willie's pickup roar out of the driveway.

"It ain't true, Mama, what Sarah Louise said! I get scared when I'm up in front of all those people. I wouldn't do it except that I know God wants me to be a healer. I was just happy 'cause the blind girl got healed."

Mama got off the sofa and knelt before me. She pulled my hands off my ears and held them in her own. "I believe ya, Esta Lea. I think Sarah Louise is just jealous. She's the one with big dreams of glory. That girl worries me." Mama heaved a heavy sigh. "But you do need to know, sweetie pie, that healers can get all puffed up and full of pride. Being around all that power can do something to ya. It's been the downfall of many."

"I don't think you need to worry about that, Mama. God told me if He could use a donkey, He could use me."

Mama laughed. "That's a humbling thought. Sounds like you are getting to know God. Just keep listening."

*　*　*

The next night was Daddy's night off, so he took me out for a cheeseburger at the local diner, the Drive-In. It was our special date night, where I talked and he listened. He used to have them with Sarah Louise, but she had too many real dates now and didn't have time for Daddy dates.

News of the healing of Althea Reynolds had spread like gravy on Nana's best white tablecloth. As soon as my foot crossed the threshold of the Drive-In, the hubbub died down to a murmur. My ears blazed so red, they probably matched my hair. Aunt Phoebe Eileen stopped talking in her normal honking voice and began to whisper. She and Uncle Farley stared at me, and Uncle Farley cleared his throat twice. It was like they were trying to see something new in me and couldn't. They didn't even say hello. I felt like telling them to look down my throat and into my ears and up my nose while they were at it. Maybe they could find something new there.

My cousin Adele was sitting with them. She waved and yelled, "Oooh, can I touch you, Esta Lea?"

"Put a lid on it, Adele," I told her. And then I said, "Daddy, I didn't bargain on being famous."

Before he could answer, the waitress stopped at our table. "Can I get y'all something?"

"Two cheeseburger plates and two chocolate shakes," Daddy replied.

"And bring a whole bottle of catsup. I love those fries," I said.

"Honey," Daddy said after she left, "in answer to your comment, it's just the way of people. They're always looking for something to worship. Can you remember Althea Reynolds's face after she got healed?"

"Yes." A warm sensation filled me.

"You just keep remembering that. This whole thing is about loving God and loving other people. Trust God, Esta Lea. He's got your best at heart."

"But trusting ain't easy, Daddy."

"It's a learning thing, Esta Lea. Are you struggling to trust God?"

"No," I said, "I'm struggling to trust Peter Earl."

"Well, that's understandable, him being your fun-loving, troublesome uncle, but I do believe he's saved now, and Uncle Bentley and the elders are watching him. You got enough to do just watching and listening to God."

"Okay, Daddy."

The waitress put our plates in front of us. Daddy prayed and then took a bite of his cheeseburger. I drank my shake and poured a huge pool of catsup in the center of my plate. I dipped the French fries in it and licked my fingers after each bite. I was gonna be too full for the cheeseburger.

When I finished the fries, I looked up and saw Sky peering over the red-faded-to-rust curtain in the front window. "I got to go, Daddy! I'll see you at home. Here." I handed him my cheeseburger. "I'm stuffed." Then I quick-kissed him on the cheek.

"I saw y'all's truck over here so I peeked in, hoping you'd be here," Sky said as we walked along Main Street. "Lewis is fixing our truck, so let's sit here on the sidewalk in front of the pharmacy where I can see the garage. Patsy told me about the healing when Daddy and I came in for his pills yesterday. Is it true? Patsy wouldn't lie to me about the healing of a blind girl, but it's hard to believe."

"It's true. All I can say is that you were right, Sky. God can use a person who ain't perfect. God told me that if He could use a donkey, He could use me. I heard it like it was my nana yelling into my ear in her deaf days."

"Wow, you are a healer! It's as clear as the

freckles on your face, Esta Lea. You may get to be a saint yet."

"When it comes to saints, you're way ahead of me, Sky Shorts, so I don't want to hear any more about it. The person I'm worried about when it comes to sainthood is Peter Earl. I'm not positive, but I think he stole the offering in Chancellor."

"Took it all for himself, you mean?"

"Yep. It was supposed to go to a missionary fund there at the church, but he didn't even give it to the deacons or pastor."

"Maybe he was going to mail it," Sky said. After taking one look at the pickled-up, unbelieving expression on my face, she added, "Or take it over to them later, somehow."

"I guess I'll give him the benefit of good thoughts for the moment. Daddy said I needed to learn to trust."

Just then Patsy poked her head out the pharmacy door and said, "Do y'all want a Coca-Cola?"

"I left my money at home," I said.

"This one's on me." Patsy brought out two Cokes. They were so cold, they must have been in the fridge in her office.

"Nice color," I said, referring to Patsy's hair.

Her teased-up hair was deep brown and flipped up right at her neckline. "Is it a new rinse?"

"Yes. Glad you like it. I think I'll keep it for a while." Most ladies just covered their gray with a blackish rinse, but Patsy had tried that one and moved on. She used every new hair thing that came into the pharmacy. She changed her hair as often as my mama changed the furniture around, which was every couple of months. She'd even peroxided her hair. "Blondened," my daddy called it.

"As soon as I'm allowed, I'm coloring my hair," I said to Sky and Patsy. "Then I'm peroxiding it."

"I take back what I said about you becoming a saint," said Sky. "I ain't never read about a blondened saint."

Chapter Ten

Overcomers

In the world ye shall have tribulation: but be of
good cheer; I have overcome the world.

John 16:33

"Esta Lea," Peter Earl called out from the backyard, "where are you?" I ran outside to see him
standing there in patched jeans, work boots, and a
sweat-stained T-shirt. He had a shovel in his hand.
He had told Daddy he'd mend the fence around the
garden about a year ago. Maybe that's what he was
doing now.

"We got a meeting tonight at the Mighty in Spirit Church in Mahoney County," Peter Earl said.

"Speaking of meetings, what happened to the offering money in Chancellor?"

"Now, Esta Lea, what kind of question is that?"

"A good one. Seeing you return empty-handed just got me to thinking. Maybe you and the monkey were in cahoots. You have to admit that he had good timing. By the time you got back in, nobody remembered the offering or the monkey."

"My, my, what an imagination you have! I assure you, that offering is in a safe place."

"Oh, I'm sure of that, but where is the safe place? In the church's missionary offering fund?"

"Esta Lea, this ain't your business."

"I know, but it is the Lord's business."

"That's right. Now let Him take care of it."

"Peter Earl, I got my eye on you. Don't you go messing up God's healing crusades."

Peter Earl threw down the shovel. "You are straining my patience. I got to get cleaned up. I'll be back a little before supper. We're going over to Chancellor to pick up Dora. We'll eat at June's." He huffed away.

I sighed. Dora again! She was getting to be a regular fixture in Peter Earl's life, kinda like dentures. I headed up to my room to change.

Sarah Louise and I were ready when we heard the rattle of Peter Earl's pickup. She was over her tantrum by now and speaking to me again. Her fits were like Carolina thunderstorms, showy and short-lived. I never took them too seriously, but that was probably 'cause she hadn't spawned a tornado yet.

"I got this feeling, Esta Lea. Tonight is the night. Destiny," she whispered as we drove off. I nodded in agreement. I had the prickles in my scalp, and I knew they were for her.

"Peter Earl, I've been wondering about something since the last church meeting," I said.

"What is it now? I don't know how your mama and daddy put up with you, Esta Lea. You got more questions than a hoot owl."

"Well, this is a simple one. What was the free gift you promised all those people?"

"Oh, that's easy—the free gift of salvation."

"You got all those people down there with a promise of a free gift, and you were going to tell them it was salvation?"

"Yep, you got it."

"That red-faced man might have killed you," I said.

"Yep. It's a good thing the Lord came through and took his mind off of it."

"Peter Earl, you better watch out. You were a salesman, but now you're a preacher."

"You need some new tactics," Sarah Louise threw in.

We rolled up in front of June's right then. Peter Earl's pickup made a *slam-putt* sound before it shut off. Dora must have heard it because she was there at the screen door wiggling her fingers and saying, "Y'all come on in. Sit down right here." She put us in front of the window like we were honored guests and brought out ham, black-eyed peas, and biscuits. Then she sat down and pursed her lips, which also tightened her eyes.

"I got something to tell y'all. Right before you came, there was a bunch of college kids here. They sat down right over there"—she pointed to a table in the corner—"and they said they was coming to the meeting to make sure that nothing happened at the church tonight. They said they don't want no more religion here. They like the town the way it is. They're probably just bored and looking for something to do. But it sounds like trouble in the service. What will y'all do?" Her voice rose and ended on a quiver. She leaned over the table toward Peter Earl and grabbed his forearm and squeezed it. I closed my eyes 'cause I was afraid that something would spill out of her blouse. I didn't want my meal ruined by excess.

Sarah Louise was staring out the window with that moon-eyed look on her face, which meant she hadn't heard anything beyond the words "college-age boys."

"Well, now, I'm sure the Holy Ghost will show us what to do, Dora. We had a monkey last time, and we'll have morons this time," Peter Earl said.

Here we go, I thought, the powers of evil are coming up against us, just like they came up against the heroes in the Bible. "Lord," I silently prayed, "I hope You know what to do, and I hope You let us in on it. I trust You, but I'm not trusting Peter Earl, or Sarah Louise, and certainly not Dora when it comes to defeating evil. Help."

We drove over to Townham with Dora squished

in the pickup with us. Her gardenia-scented per-fume made me dizzy. I coughed right up to the time I stumbled out of the pickup.

I hoped the church lived up to its name and had a mighty spirit, 'cause its body was a squat concrete block square that looked like somebody had plopped it down sideways on a slab of concrete. It even had an off-center steeple. I opened the church door, and there they were—the visitors.

"Why, you must be the healer!" one cultured drunken voice called out from up front with a pure-t uppity rich folks' accent. Sarah Louise strained to see who had that voice.

"Well now, if there is one thing I recognize, it is the sound and smell of whiskey," Peter Earl said.

"Hello, preacher man. Where are my manners? We were passing through so we thought we'd drop by." A young man stood up. He had blond wavy hair and was wearing a disheveled white suit. He brushed his hair off his forehead, walked toward us, and put out his hand to shake Peter Earl's.

Peter Earl shook it and said, "We're glad you came. Feel free to stick around awhile." I turned to look at Sarah Louise 'cause I knew what I'd find there. Yep, her entranced eyes spelled "D-E-S-T-I-N-Y." She pushed past me and pranced up front.

"I'm Sarah Louise Ridley. Pleased to meet you." She stuck out her hand like she was waiting for a shake.

"I'm Jefferson Howard Scott, but you can call me Jefferson. Pleased to meet you, Sarah Louise." He took her hand, pulled it to his mouth, and kissed it. I expected Sarah Louise to faint, but she didn't.

The platform was beautified with Southern Comfort, Jack Daniel's, and Wild Turkey. It looked pretty if you closed one eye, tilted your head, and winked at it, which is what I imagine these folks must have been doing when they put the bottles up there.

There were two girls on the second bench smoking Lucky Strikes. I immediately thought of the brown-haired one as Lucky and the red-haired one as Strike. A couple of men sat on the floor in front of the platform playing poker. One was smoking a cigar.

A man with broad cheekbones, a jutting nose, and a flat head ran into the church. He looked like an anvil in a bunchy black suit. "I guess y'all have met our newcomers," he said, glancing at the college kids up front. I saw that the back of his head was flat too.

Peter Earl stepped forward.

"Hello. I'm Peter Earl Jewels, and these are my nieces Sarah Louise Ridley and Esta Lea Ridley."

"Oh, pardon me, where are my manners? I forgot myself. I'm Pastor Asa Robbins. Welcome to the Mighty in Spirit Church."

"Whiskey is good for the sinuses. Did you know that, Pastor Robbins?" said one of the poker players.

"Just ignore them, Pastor Robbins. I'll take care of them," Peter Earl said.

The church began filling up from the back to the front. Nana came in, with Aunt Opal close behind her. They sat right behind Lucky and Strike, but no one else wanted to sit close to the college kids. The last people to come in were Ezra Samples, the deaf boy who'd been at the last service, and his family. "Oh, Lord," I prayed when I saw them, "overcome the evil doings for their sakes."

Energy crackled in the air. I couldn't tell if it was the force between the college folks and the church folks or if it was a real thunderstorm. Then I heard a peal of thunder rolling in from a long ways away.

"Hello, y'all. We are doing things differently

tonight. I know that all of y'all are here for some Gospel power in the evening hour," Pastor Robbins began.

"Hour, tower," came from a poker player.

"Tower, power," came from another.

"Power, sour," came from a third.

Jefferson didn't say anything. His eyes were on the platform. They were fixed on Sarah Louise Ridley. That man would be leaving this meeting with a new purpose.

"So I will get on with introducing our guests without any further interruptions," said Pastor Robbins.

"That's what you think," Lucky yelled.

"We're just getting started," Strike yelled.

"No need to introduce us, Pastor," Peter Earl said as we went up to the platform. He stood at the pulpit and stared out at the crowd. "Let's take up the special overseas missionary offering as I get started here." The ushers passed the plates.

Peter Earl's face slid into its best salesman lines, and he said, "Did y'all hear the one about the atheist? A famous preacher named Aimee Semple McPherson told it years ago."

"No!" Lucky and Strike yelled.

"Well, seems there was this atheist who died. His family had him laid out just fine. The whole neighborhood trouped through for the viewing. One of the neighbors leaned over and looked into the casket and remarked to the undertaker, 'Oh, poor man! He doesn't believe in heaven, and he doesn't believe in hell. He's all dressed up with nowhere to go.' "

The college kids roared and called for more. "Here's another," Peter Earl said, "taken from a church bulletin in North Carolina. Well, a fine funeral was ordered for a woman who had hen-pecked her husband, driven her kids to drink, sparred with the neighbors whenever possible, and even made her cat and dog crazy. She had a violent temper, you see. As the casket was lowered into the grave, a fierce thunderstorm broke, and the pastor's benediction was overpowered by a blinding flash of lightning, followed by terrific thunder. 'Well,' commented one of the neighbors, 'she got there all right.' "

All those years of sitting in pews, listening to revival preachers' jokes and stories had not been wasted on Peter Earl. He was in fine form, slicker than spit and quicker than a critter in hunting season. A few jokes later and the cigar smoker was asleep and snoring, but Jefferson and the other poker players were listening. Lucky and Strike weren't smoking anymore.

Peter Earl went on.

"A funny thing happened to me on my way to church one night. I got dead drunk, hit the porch post, and ended up face-down on my sister's front porch. Has that ever happened to any of you?"

"Close enough," one of the poker players answered. "I got dead drunk and peed on an electrified fence on my way home."

"Oh my," I heard one woman say. I saw her try to cover her son's ears.

"Now, when I say 'on my way to church,' I don't mean directly," Peter Earl went on. "I mean the indirect, roundabout way. Through lots of bars, towns, and years. I was convinced that the church had nothing to say to me. I saw the hypocrisy of folks and used it as an excuse for not having much to do with God.

"But that drunken night when I woke up at my sister's house, I saw the healing power of the Lord. He anointed my niece Esta Lea. She touched my mama, and my mama was healed of her deafness. It was a miracle. No more excuses for me. I decided that my days of sinning were over. I saw the light."

People were listening. Peter Earl turned to me and said, "Why don't you take over from here, Esta Lea."

I stared at him. "Are you crazy? I ain't never preached before."

Peter Earl walked over, took my hand, and pulled me up out of my seat. He whispered, "Shhh, you'll do just fine." He led me to the pulpit, placed my hands on either side of it, and murmured, "Hold on for dear life." Then he sat down.

I closed my eyes and took a deep breath. When I opened my eyes, the words just flowed out: "Listen up, Mighty in Spirit Church. When Jesus preached His first sermon He said, 'The Spirit of the Lord has anointed me to preach the gospel to the poor. He has sent me to heal the brokenhearted, to preach deliverance to the captives and recovery of sight to the blind.' " I paused to catch my breath. "Are you with me, church?" I felt like I was watching myself up there behind the pulpit.

"Yes," Lucky said.

"Preach it, Esta Lea!" Nana yelled.

"Come on!" Aunt Opal yelled.

"I tell you, the very same Jesus is here tonight, and He still has the power to heal the brokenhearted and the blind, and to deliver you and me from hell."

The room was still, but the energy level was magnified. A flash of lightning with a clap of thunder right on top of it split the air.

"Lord, Lord," Asa Robbins said.

Dora was dumbstruck. Her mouth hung open at a slant. She was tilted forward, her hands under her thighs, as if she was trying to perch herself higher.

"And so I leave you with the question, do you know this Jesus?" Another crash of lightning filled the windows. Lucky was quietly crying up front.

"If you want to know Him, come up front and we'll pray with you." I sat down, tuckered out but full of peace. It had happened, just like I'd felt it on the day of my calling. I'd stood in a pulpit and preached with the wind of the spirit and the fire of God.

"Sarah Louise, stand up and sing!" Peter Earl said.

Sarah Louise stood up. She was wearing Dora's suit and looked grown-up and somehow gentle at the same time. "Softly and tenderly, Jesus is calling, calling for you and for me," she sang slowly. She reached her gloved hands toward the pews and beckoned people forward.

Lucky jumped from her seat and knelt at the altar railing. Two of the poker players quickly followed her. Pastor Robbins went up and prayed with the men, and I went and dropped on my knees next to Lucky.

"I'm sick of it all," she said. "I want a new life."

"Just tell Jesus that," I said, so she did. She stood up with tears rolling down her smiling face.

Sarah Louise began to sing, "There's a new name written down in glory, and it's mine, oh yes, it's mine." She started clapping.

Nana and Aunt Opal got to their feet and sang and clapped along with Sarah Louise. Other people soon followed them. Then Ezra and his daddy came forward, and I prayed for Ezra again, but nothing happened.

Sarah Louise finished the song and went down to the first pew to talk to Jefferson Howard Scott. I'm sure it wasn't about salvation.

The altar was crowded. "Thank you, Jesus!"

Pastor Asa called out over and over as we prayed, cried, and sang.

At the tail end of the evening, when just about everyone else had left, a man came forward. His name was Jabez, and he was a TV repairman. He asked me to pray for him and then listed his ailments. My faith fell through a crack in the floor. He limped 'cause one leg was shorter than the other, and he had a crooked shoulder and bent back that made him look like a hunchback. And that was just the outside stuff. The inside stuff was just as bad.

Finally, when he finished, I prayed a quick "Lord, heal this man." I couldn't even remember the ailments to list them.

Nothing happened to him. He limped out the back door.

I felt a sadness descend and wrap around my shoulders like one of Nana's shawls. People were being saved, but no one was being healed. I sat down in the front row. Winford Samples came over with Ezra and squeezed my shoulder. "Look. Look what God is doing," he said. "Isn't it marvelous?"

I looked at this man whose son was still deaf, and I wondered how he could say such a thing, but there was no doubt in my mind that he meant it. He saw what God was doing, not what He wasn't.

My faith grew one size that night, but I knew it would be a long time before it filled Winford Samples's boots.

Chapter Eleven

The Lord's Army

~

For the battle is not yours, but God's.

2 Chronicles 20:15

It was the next weekend. I couldn't wait to see the Faith and Love Deliverance Tabernacle.

"A tabernacle is different from a church," I told Sarah Louise. "It will be big, fancy, and have lots of stained glass."

"No, it won't," Sarah Louise said as we bumped along on roads that kept getting smaller and smaller, going from blacktop to gravel. Finally we drove down a clay track with pine trees crowding it. The church at the end was small and plain, with no stained glass, but it did have a gigantic tent behind it. Cars and trucks were parked every which way. People were swarming to the tent like mosquitoes to a patch of bare neck.

The tent meant that the meeting was going to be muggy and hot, so I asked God to let the wind of His Spirit blow. And He did. The moment I stepped under the tent, I felt the air buzzing with Holy Ghost excitement.

At the front of the tent was a platform with a big wooden cross behind it. There wasn't any kind of pulpit, but there were three folding chairs and an organ over to one side. I bet it had taken a heap of muscle to get that thing out here. I could see a cord snaking back to the church.

A woman in an olive green dress that looked like an army pup tent was playing the organ with her feet, her black shoes hammering the pedals. It reminded me of Uncle Bentley stomping on the devil. Maybe she was stomping on the devil too. Her hair was black-and-gray streaked and she wore it up in a braided bun. The bun wobbled with each stomp, but it didn't slide off. She had happy wrinkles around her eyes and gray pouches under them. On anyone else this would have been a tired face, but not on her.

She left the organ and came over, shaking hands with each of us.

"Mighty good of y'all to come. We been looking forward to this evening for a while. I'm Sister Peggy, the General of this Army, and Jesus is our Commander in Chief." She turned toward the cross and saluted. She looked around at us, so we saluted too.

Sister Peggy motioned us to the platform and she went back to the organ. She started singing, "Onward, Christian soldiers, marching as to war, with the cross of Jesus going on before. Christ the royal Master leads against the foe. Forward into battle, see His banners go." Her voice was low and hardy.

After the first verse, she asked the church to join her. People jumped to their feet and sang. She directed everyone with her hands, played the organ with her feet, and sang. Three things at one time. I was awed.

I looked around for Daddy and Uncle Bentley while we sang the first number. Sarah Louise was looking around too, but when I waved at Daddy, she nodded in the other direction. Jefferson Howard Scott was standing there with his arms crossed.

So that was where Sarah Louise had been five nights out of seven nights last week! Her non-Jefferson reasons for going out had fooled even me.

After the first hymn, Sarah Louise went to the front of the platform and led the singing like a choir director. After we finished the singing, the ushers collected the mission's offering. The baskets were overflowing with money. Peter Earl took them and walked out the back of the tent.

While Sarah Louise was singing a special number, Peter Earl returned to the platform. Just then a man drove his car right up to the back of the tent. He tooted his horn and jumped out of the car and danced, skipped, twirled, whooped, and hollered down the center aisle. When he got close to the front, he did a handspring up onto the platform. Sarah Louise jumped off the platform and ran toward Jefferson. The man pulled me off my chair and twirled me around.

"Whoa, whoa! What's going on here?" Peter Earl asked. Daddy had jumped up from his seat too.

The man dropped my arms and said, "You

don't recognize me, do you?" Before I could answer, he spun around to Peter Earl and said, "She don't recognize me." He turned back to me and said, "I'm the repairman. The TV repairman you prayed for in Townham."

Only one TV repairman came to my mind, and this wasn't him. That repairman limped and looked like a hunchback. Only if I took away the hard face, limp, and hunch was there a resemblance. The man laughed.

It was the repairman! But he was healed! Completely.

"How did this happen?" I asked. "When I prayed for you, nothing changed."

"That's right," he said, and turned to the crowd. "When she prayed for me, nothing happened, so I went back home. I had a hunched shoulder, gimpy leg, bunched-up intestines, high blood pressure, and diabetes. But that night in bed a warmth covered me, and then a shaking. It started with my shoulder and went through my whole body. It lasted all night. In the morning, I was healed. God healed everything. Hallelujah. Hallelujah!" The crowd cheered and clapped. It grew to a roar.

Sister Peggy ran to the platform. Sweat flew off

her arms as she waved them. She whistled. It was a fingers-in-the-mouth, loud-enough-to-stop-the-cheering whistle, but she did it without the fingers. This woman was great! "Lord, let me be like Sister Peggy someday," I prayed under my breath.

"Brothers and Sisters. While we were cheering, the Lord showed me that we are the Army of Praise and Worship. We will march around this tent, and the Lord will defeat the enemy like He did in the days of Israel when Jehoshaphat was the king of Judah. Jehoshaphat called out to the Lord because the enemy was coming against him. God said the battle was His, so Jehoshaphat put the praisers in front of the army. When they got to the battlefield, the Lord defeated the enemy—" Shouts of "Hallelujah!" and "Glory!" interrupted her. "That old enemy, the evil one, will be defeated tonight, and many will be healed."

We all moved outside the tent. Sister Peggy and Jabez led the way as people skipped, danced, sang, shouted, and prayed in tongues. You name it, it happened. We circled the tent twice and then went back inside. Sister Peggy shouted, "All you who need healing come to the front." She motioned to Peter Earl and me to join her on the platform. Sarah Louise wasn't around. I wondered if she was with Jefferson.

"For He has borne our iniquities and healed our diseases!" shouted Sister Peggy. "Beloved, beloved God is here in a mighty way this night. There is healing power all around. There is an anointing..." And *boom,* she fell over on the platform.

Boom, boom, Peter Earl and I fell back into the folding chairs. It was like a giant hand had pushed us.

The air was tight around me, and I was panting like a dog. Peter Earl was gasping for breath. His chest heaved and his eyes bulged. I wanted to laugh, but I didn't have the air. Sister Peggy staggered up, and cries of "Hallelujah," "Praise God," "Amen, Sister" came from all over the tent.

People poured up front. "We need all the healers to pray, and all the praisers to praise!" shouted Sister Peggy.

She motioned to Peter Earl, Jabez, and me. I knew that Peter Earl didn't think he was a healer, but after being winded by the breath of God, I guess he wasn't arguing. Then Daddy and Uncle Bentley joined us too.

Right in front of me were Winford Samples and Ezra.

"This is the boy I told you about at supper last week, Daddy," I said. I laid my hands on Ezra's ears and shouted because the praisers were so loud. "Lord, You know the faith of Ezra's daddy, You know that he loves You, and he won't be mad at You if nothing happens, but he still wants his little boy to be healed."

Ezra dropped to his knees and covered his ears with his hands. He was crying. Winford dropped to his knees and held his son. Ezra's tears were wetting his daddy's shirt.

"Ezra," he said, "is it too loud?" He signed while he talked.

Ezra nodded, and Winford picked him up, hugging him tight. "Hallelujah, hallelujah, he's healed! My boy is healed!" I had to lean in to hear Winford because there was so much noise. "Thank you, Esta, and thank you, Jesus! I'm gonna take Ezra home to tell his mama and brothers and sisters now. Goodbye, Esta Lea. If I don't see you again before heaven, God bless you real good."

"He has, Mr. Samples. He let me know you and Ezra," I said. They walked out of the tent.

A pang of joy shot down through me. It went so deep, it hurt. The rest of the evening was a blur of praying.

When the meeting was over, Uncle Bentley, Daddy, and I drove home. I kept falling asleep and waking up. I remember Daddy saying that Sarah Louise was coming home with Peter Earl. Something was niggling my mind. When we got home, Daddy put his arm around my waist and half carried me up to bed.

"The offerings," I whispered to him, and then I fell asleep with my clothes on.

Chapter Twelve

The Lord Speaks

With men of other tongues and other lips
will I speak unto this people.
1 Corinthians 14:21

It was the next weekend. Sarah Louise and I stood at
the back of the Shiloh Springs Evangelistic Church
of Deliverance after the Sunday morning service.
We were greeting people with side-to-side hugs,
A-frame hugs, and some pat-pats on the back for
good measure.

Peter Earl stood next to us doing the handshake thing. He was good at it. Make no mistake, he was Ruby Irene's born-and-carried-into-the-church son, even if he hadn't darkened the church's doors for years. He'd size up people as they walked up and decide whether to do the shake-shake-pull hand-shake, the shake with the right hand while patting on the upper arm with the left hand, or the kiss of brotherly love. The kiss was reserved for women—permed, purple-tinted women.

That's when I saw her, the "Lord have mercy" woman. "Lord, have mercy and hide us quick, before that woman gets to us," Sarah Louise and I prayed whenever we saw one, and then we'd look for the quickest way out of the church. There's at least two of these women in every church. They seem to head up the important committees.

"I can see you got the touch of the Lord, Sister," said the big-haired woman. She waited for me to look into her eyes, but I couldn't stop looking at her hair. It was teased and shellacked into a beehive of immense size, with a little pink rose tucked in the top. Maybe the rose was there to attract the bees, or maybe it was there to match her mauve lips. Could be it was there to match her dress. Her massive bosom was covered with mauve roses on a yellow background. The blossoms heaved mightily with the weight of her words.

"You got to do something about my mama. She ain't right in the head. Ever since my daddy died, she's been clean off her rocker. She's always been a bit headstrong—doing what she wanted, when she wanted, and not taking no for an answer. Why, her favorite saying is 'Ain't nobody's business but my own.' Now she won't leave the house. She won't come to church. She sits out on the front porch staring at the heap of junk growing in the front yard. It's the most shameful thing."

Shameful for who? I wondered.

"Lord have mercy," Sarah Louise said, dipping her head as she did so.

"Yes, yes, Lord have mercy and heal my mama," the woman went on. "Calls her junk heap 'the Living History Repository.' Sounds indecent, doesn't it? Can you believe it?"

"Ma'am." I jumped in as she caught her breath. "I'd be happy to visit your mama. How about tomorrow morning?" The Living History Repository sounded too good to miss.

That's when I felt Peter Earl's arm go 'round my shoulder. He squeezed it hard.

"I believe we'll be on the road by that time, ma'am," he said. "So sorry. The Lord will send some other minister along. He hears the cries of his saints."

I stared at him. "We'll stop by this afternoon," I said.

"We'll be there," Sarah Louise said.

"Praise God. Glory. I'm obliged to you," said the woman. "Go to the edge of town and turn right on Flatbed Road. Turn left at the first lane you see. Keep going until you see her place. It's the only one down there."

"I ain't going with you. I got other plans for this afternoon," Peter Earl said after she walked away.

After dinner Sarah Louise and I walked to the edge of town. You couldn't miss it. Two white houses faced each other across Main Street, and then there weren't any more. In the yard of one house a battered green street sign read FLATBED ROAD. In the other yard a sign read CITY LIMITS.

We turned and walked on a gravel road until we

saw a lane. A large tree stood on either side of it, and two grooves cracked the red clay. Palmetto pines and scrubby firs were covered with creeping vine. As we walked, the air got thick, heavy with honeysuckle. I yawned, and it was only two in the afternoon.

We went around a curve and there it was: the Living History Repository. Sarah Louise and I stood in silence. Even the birds were quiet as we tried to take it all in.

A car skeleton at the edge of the woods sprouted weeds. A telephone pole carved like a totem pole stuck out of the car window. The concrete pedestal to a birdbath lay across an old four-wheeled baby carriage. There was no sign of the birdbath basin, but there was a blue gazing ball with a large crack. A maroon recliner with cotton stuffing coming out of the seams cradled a huge piece of driftwood. Both were tossed on top of a brown vinyl sofa covered with cracks. A wringer washer with a TV antenna sticking out of it stood beside a huge pile of concrete blocks. A real stop sign leaned on the blocks.

Windmill whirligigs and aluminum pie tins tied to sticks were planted here and there among the treasures. To keep the crows away, I imagined.

There was more, but my eyes were too tired to see it all.

Then I heard it, the *creak, creak* of a rocker on wood. We were being watched from the porch by a tiny old woman. A pair of black eyes peered out of her wrinkles. Wisps of gray strayed from under the red bandanna on her head. A thin gray braid lay across her shoulder. She was wearing a house-dress faded beyond color with little black flowers sprinkled here and there. Her apron and dress nearly covered her feet and hands. Either she had shrunk or the clothes had grown. Sturdy black shoes poked out from under the apron.

"Morning, ma'am," Sarah Louise called.

"Welcome, welcome. I'm Mama Merrilee," she replied. "What brings y'all out here on this glorify-ing morning? Not too many folks stray down my lane." Her voice was sweet and full. Seemed funny coming from such a shriveled woman.

"Heard you had a museum out here," I said. "We were at the Evangelistic Church of Deliver-ance this morning, and we learned about it there. They're having special services."

"Yeah, I heard. Believe me, with a daughter like mine, you hear. Come on in. I was baking this morning while it was cool. Y'all are in time for my chocolate tarts. My daughter is coming by later on to pick some up. You can tell me how they taste."

Sarah Louise and I wandered through the rubble and followed the woman through the screen door. She clumped when she walked. The thick aroma of chocolate filled the house. It looked like Mama Merrilee did most of her living in the kitchen. It was crammed with a table, chairs, a recliner, an old hutch, and a washing machine with an old brown RCA radio on top of it. You could barely pull the chairs out.

"Truth-telling time. Did my daughter send y'all out?" Mama Merrilee asked.

"She wanted us to come, but I came 'cause I wanted to see all your stuff. You have more junk than anyone. It's great," I said.

"Esta!" Sarah Louise hissed. "Where are your manners?"

Mama Merrilee didn't seem to mind. She laughed long and loud, then grabbed my hand and said, "Kindred spirits."

"Kindred spirits," I answered.

"Each of those things out there has a special

meaning to me. When I sit on my porch, I look down and call up a memory. These memories lead me to people and places all over. Then I pray for those folks. Pick something out," she said, and looked at me.

"The stop sign."

"Ah, now that's a sad one. That's the first thing my son Eli ever stole. Decorated his clubhouse with it. Sad to say, he stole many more things. Cars were his favorite thing to steal. He ended up in jail over in Alabama. Still there. When I look at that stop sign, I pray for him. He needs it. You know, I probably pray around the world every day. I'm quite a world traveler even though I can't do much on account of these legs." She pulled up her skirt and showed us her braces. "Gimpy legs plus old age means stay put. Besides I can't get around unless my daughter drives me. I love my daughter, but I can only take her in small doses."

We sat at the table and ate chocolate tarts. They were heavenly. Mama Merrilee couldn't be crazy if she could cook like that. I asked for another one. It was as good as the first. She made us some tea, and we talked about some of her favorite memories. It was getting to be time to head back, so I stood up.

"I bet my daughter told you I was crazy as a coot." Mama Merrilee looked at Sarah Louise, who reddened. She couldn't answer.

Then Mama Merrilee looked at me. "Yes, she did," I said. "She wanted us to pray for you."

"And do you want to pray for me?"

"Yes, but not because you are crazy. I just want to bless you," I said.

"Well, go right ahead."

"God, thank you for Mama Merrilee. She's doing your work and I'm glad. Bless her real good."

She looked at me and said, "And how about I pray for you?"

"Sure," I said.

"Lord, bless this girl. You have a calling on her life. Don't let her forget that." She stopped and looked right at me and said, "The Lord has a word for you: 'Don't forget the clock and watch. Wait for God's time.'"

It was my dream, my dream about Peter Earl! I stared at her and said, "Are you a prophetess like Anna in the Bible?"

"Some have said so," she answered.

"Well, I know so." I leaned forward and kissed her on the cheek. "There was only one way you could have known about the calling and the clocks, and that's if God told you Himself, because I sure didn't."

Chapter Thirteen

Redeeming Time

~

See then that ye walk circumspectly,
not as fools, but as wise,
Redeeming the time, because the days are evil.

Ephesians 5:15–16

The sunlight danced among the leaves, making shadows on my wall. Mama must have let me sleep late because of all the meetings we'd been going to. I put my pillow over my head and tried to go back to sleep, but I couldn't.

I thought about what Mama Merrilee had said about the clocks and waiting for God's time. I knew it meant I had to get out of the healing crusade business because Peter Earl wasn't ready to be a preacher yet. It wasn't God's time for me to be doing crusades. Now I was sure he was stealing the offerings. But where was he putting them? Our town was so small, if he put them in the bank, someone was bound to notice.

"Esta Lea, Sky just called and said to meet her at the usual place," my mama called upstairs.

I got dressed quick and raced downtown on my bike.

"It's been a million years since I last saw you, Sky Shorts."

"At least! Where were you last night?"

"At the Shiloh Springs Evangelistic Church of Deliverance. Sarah Louise and I visited a prophetess who keeps junk in her front yard. Each piece is a memory that helps her pray."

"Wow! A shrine. A holy place like Lourdes. Was her name Bernadette? That would be too good."

"Sorry, it's Mama Merrilee, but she is a prophetess. She prayed this for me, 'Lord, bless this girl. You have a calling on her life. Don't let her forget that.' Then she told me the Lord has a special word for me—not to forget the clock and watch, and to wait for God's time." I told Sky the timing dream. "What do you think about Mama Merrilee's word?"

"It's obvious, Esta. You have a calling, and you were right about Peter Earl. You need to tell someone about him."

"I already talked to Nana and Daddy about Peter Earl, and they seemed to think he's changed. Patsy Ann wasn't too sure he'd changed, but she didn't think it mattered."

"What you need is proof," Sky said.

"Yeah, you're right. I've got to find those offerings."

"Come on," Sky said. "Let's walk toward the hardware store."

"Okay, as long as we don't go in." My mind was too full of other things. Willie Boyd's daddy owned the store and Willie worked there. I knew I didn't have space for him right then.

But Sky pushed open the screen door and went into the store, calling over her shoulder, "Come on, Esta Lea. We ain't got all day."

"How are y'all?" Willie asked. "Can I help you with something, Esta Lea?" I groaned at the sound of Willie's voice.

"I was thinking of buying some nails," Sky said. She grinned at me over her shoulder and followed Willie toward the cubbies full of nails.

The ladders were right next to me, so I stared at them.

"Do you need a hand with a ladder, Esta Lea?" asked Willie.

"No, not really. It's just a passing fancy," I said. Willie steadied my arm as I tripped over a hollow in the wooden floor. My cheeks flamed up and burned my freckles.

"I never did get a chance to tell you that I admired what you did for Billy Oaks at that revival meeting," Willie said. "My life was changed that day. It will never be the same."

Someone must have drilled a hole in my brain and let the words drain out, 'cause they were gone.

"Hmm," I stammered.

"Thanks," Sky hissed.

"Thanks," I said.

"I ain't been out to y'all's place lately. Sarah Louise broke up with me two weeks ago."

"Yes, well . . . ," I said.

"Got to get going," Sky said. "Bye."

"Bye," I echoed, and followed Sky out the door.

She ran around the corner and sat down on the sidewalk. "Passing fancy, my foot," she said, and laughed fit to be tied. But then she got more sympathetic, in her usual way. "Too bad about Willie Boyd. You been liking him forever and a day. But you got to give it up, Esta Lea. He's still sweet on Sarah Louise. You will remind him of his broken heart. Toss him in the rubbish heap of your mind."

"My feelings don't always do what they are told." I'd heard enough talking about Willie, so I said, "Let's go over to the square."

We headed over to Robert E. Lee, with his green feet and bird fans. Pulling my sticky shirt off my back and kicking my sandals off felt good. Sky looked cool as always. We plopped on the grass, and Sky picked clover flowers.

"Sarah Louise is seeing a college boy named Jefferson Howard Scott," I said. "She met him at one of our meetings. He's all the things she wants: rich, good looking, and talks nicelike."

"Don't tell me," Sky said. She stood up and let her hair fall over her face. She spread her feet about a foot apart and placed her hands on her hips, imitating Sarah Louise. "He's not a hick, a redneck, or small-town. He's my ticket to the big time."

I laughed and said, "You have her down to a T. But we know the big question is can he get her into country music or the movies? If I were into betting, which I ain't, I wouldn't bet one red nickel on him being that good."

"When it comes to dreams, Sarah Louise ain't no different than most girls here in Beulah Land, for all her talk of the big time," Sky said. "She'll probably just marry soon."

"Well, it won't be for a while. Mama and Daddy don't even know she's dating him yet. She's keeping this one under wraps. She's afraid they won't like him 'cause he ain't saved. That's how I see it anyway. She'll go slow."

"I got to get going," Sky said. She walked over to the World War II tank and waved as her daddy came around the corner of the courthouse. Sky had an amazing sense in her knower when it came to where her daddy was.

As I rode my bike past the bank, I thought about Peter Earl and the offering money. Then I remembered him coming from the garden with the shovel in his hand. That was it! He'd buried the offering. I'd find it, and then I'd have proof! I'd just have to tell Mama and Daddy. There'd be no more meetings with Peter Earl; my calling was for some other time.

At home I downed two glasses of water, stuck my head under the water hose, and sat on the front porch to cool off.

"Esta Lea, close the door," said Mama. "We don't live in a barn. Every fly in Alamain County thinks it's open house here."

"Sorry, Mama."

"Come and get your little brother. I need you to watch him for a spell so I can get some cleaning done."

"Okay, Mama. I'll take him out to the garden." This was perfect! I could look for the money, and everyone would think I was just watching Ben.

Opening the shed door let a whoosh of blistery air out, so I held my breath, ran in, and grabbed a small shovel. I started out digging where the fence was supposed to be but found nothing. It wasn't a total waste though because Ben was having a great time. He put a clump of garden dirt in his mouth and opened his mouth to show me.

"No, Ben." I dug the dirt out. Ben smiled and wiped his dirty hands on his bare belly.

I found nothing in the harvested part of the garden where the peas and spinach had been, nothing in the green-bean rows, and nothing between the rows of corn. The shovel bounced on the ground as I sat down against the shed and wiped the sweat from my eyes.

"Esta Lea, y'all come on in. You can set the table for supper."

"Okay, Mama." I looked around, but I couldn't see Ben. He wasn't in the garden or the backyard. Baby Ben wasn't in sight anywhere.

"Mama! I can't find Ben!"

"What?" she yelled as she flew out the back door. We dashed around the backyard together, ran through the garden, and circled the house. Elijah was jumping up and down at the back screen door, barking like fury.

"Hush up, Elijah." I sat on the porch with a growing fever inside. I couldn't take Elijah's barking anymore, so I opened the back door.

Elijah bolted to the shed and ran in. A sleepy-looking Ben Ridley stumbled out. Ben lifted his arms to Mama.

"Oh, thank God!" she said as she picked Ben up

and smothered him with kisses. Ben was covered in dirt and dog slobber, but he didn't seem to mind. He laughed like he was saying *What is all the fuss about?*

"Where was your mind, Esta Lea?" said Mama. "You were supposed to be keeping an eye on him. What were you doing out here?"

"Working in the garden."

"I can see that, but when I say watch Baby Ben, that's exactly what I mean. You go up to your room for now. I'll call you down when I think you're ready."

I went upstairs and flopped on the bed. So much for telling Mama and Daddy tonight! This was definitely not a good time.

I needed some air! I yanked my window higher, but that didn't bring any breeze in. Just then I saw Sarah Louise walking—no, "prancing" is the proper word—across the yard. She looked puckered up from happiness.

"Sarah Louise," I yelled. "Come up here." She came up the stairs and into our room. "You look pleased as puddin'. What's going on?"

"Can't say."

"Come on, Sarah Louise. I ain't never told your secrets. You know that."

"I know, Esta, but I can't tell anybody this one. No one and nobody." She looked at me with an honest sweetness I couldn't figure. "And someday you'll thank me. Trust me. But what did you want me for?" She stretched with both arms above her head.

"I wanted to let you know that I'm going to tell Mama and Daddy that Peter Earl is stealing the offerings," I said.

"So what if he is, Esta Lea. Who's he stealing from, God?"

"Yes! That money is for the work of the Lord, not Peter Earl's old lottery scam or high-falutin' living or new schemes."

"When?" Sarah Louise asked.

"When what?"

"When are you going to tell them?"

"I was going to tell them tonight," I said. "But now that I'm in the doghouse, I'm going to tell them before our next meeting."

"You can't!" Sarah Louise wailed.

"I refuse to do even one more meeting with Peter Earl. What if he messes up my calling?"

"Esta Lea, you got to go!" Her voice rose to panic pitch. She put a hand on my arm.

"Why?"

"Because I have to go to this meeting tomorrow night. It's part of the secret," Sarah Louise said. She began twisting her hair into ringlets.

"If you can't tell me even a little bit, why should I do anything for you?"

"Okay, okay. It has to do with seeing Jefferson. That's all I can tell you. And, Esta, I'll owe you big. Like for the rest of my life."

Mama always said that Sarah Louise is too dramatic, and she's right. It wears me out. "Okay, one more meeting, but that's it," I said.

"Yes, yes, yes!" she gushed. "And don't worry about your calling, you silly! It's only one more meeting." She kissed me on the cheek and ran from the room.

Why would seeing Jefferson matter that much, I wondered. Didn't make sense to me, but the idea of Sarah Louise owing me for life was sweet. The first payment would be a manicure job with her red fingernail polish.

Chapter Fourteen

Temptation

～

But God is faithful, who will not suffer you
to be tempted above that ye are able.

1 Corinthians 10:13

When we drove up to the church, it was evident that
the service was going to be unusual. A hearse was
parked in front of the church. Were we supposed to
move beyond healing the blind and the deaf to rais-
ing the dead?

"With God all things are possible. With God all
things are possible," I whispered.

"Unless my eyes are deceiving me, that is a hearse parked in front of the church," Peter Earl said.

"Chalk one up to the obvious," Sarah Louise said.

"Don't start in on me now, Sarah Louise. Is this the right church?" Peter Earl looked down at his directions.

"Yoo-hoo." A woman came out of the church and wiggled her fingers at us. It was Dora in a lime green suit with a matching hat.

"This is the place," I said. "No doubt about it."

"Such a tragedy!" Dora exclaimed. "Such a sadness! The head deacon, Charlie Lowdermilk, died. It was totally unexpected. Keeled over of a heart attack when he was tending to his private business in the men's room. Can you imagine?"

I tried not to.

"It happened at work. Lowdermilk's Accounting," she went on. "He owns it. Could have been there for days without anyone finding him, this being the summer and not tax season, but thank goodness he forgot to take his lunch that day. His wife, Lozene, had to take it to him, and she found him."

"How in the world did you find all this out already?" Sarah Louise asked.

"I got here ten minutes ago."

"That explains it," I said.

"I feel like I've known Lozene all my life. We just clicked. She needed someone to talk to in her time of sadness and all. Come in and meet her."

We followed Dora into the church. The smell of lilies filled every ounce of air. "I'm not sure what all this has to do with the meeting," I whispered to Sarah Louise.

"Surely they canceled it," she whispered back.

A man suddenly appeared at Peter Earl's arm, just appeared from nowhere. It was creepy. He had black hair, and his eyebrows went clear across his face and almost covered his eyes. He wore a black suit.

"Hello, I'm Alby Webb, the pastor here. We're so glad you could come. You see, Charlie Lowdermilk died yesterday, and when we talked about canceling the healing service, Lozene wouldn't hear of it. She's Charlie's widow. 'It would be such an honor to have these famous ministers here at the funeral. Would you ask them to do the service, Pastor? I won't have it any other way.' So of course I agreed to ask you, as Lozene is not a woman to be trifled with. I mean in her time of sorrow and all." His toneless voice faded away. "She has already booked you into two cabins at the Come As You Are Motel right outside of town so that you can be here in the morning for the graveside service too."

By this time we were at the front of the church. A tall, roomy woman turned to meet us. Loops of blond hair were piled on top of her head. An energy radiated from her as she fixed her protruding brown eyes on Peter Earl. "I'm Lozene Lowdermilk." She stuck out her hand and vibrated each of ours. Then she turned toward the casket and said, "And this is my husband, Charlie Lowdermilk."

Was he going to sit up and shake our hands too? Lozene jerked around to us as if we were supposed to do something. We all stepped up to the casket and looked in.

"How do you do," I said. Sarah Louise just nodded to Mr. Lowdermilk.

Poor Mr. Lowdermilk didn't come close to filling up the coffin. There was a good half a foot above his head, below his feet, and around his sides.

"The coffin looks a little big. Was he a sickly

man?" I asked Lozene. Sarah Louise kicked me in the shin.

"Oh, no, no, but I can see why you might think so. You see, we had matching coffins made." That explained it.

"You were thinking ahead," I said.

"Yes, yes." Lozene's voice cracked. "My Charlie was a planner. A stickler for detail. He even picked out the outfit he has on. He updated it every year. Doesn't he look wonderful? Nothing but the best for Charlie. That's his new suit, a thousand dollars. His shirt is the best, as y'all can see. Aren't his diamond cuff links gorgeous? They match that diamond tie clip. That set was his favorite. The ruby cuff links were a close second. Look at his little alligator shoes. I love the thought of an alligator giving up his life for my Charlie's feet. What a sacrifice."

"I'm not sure the alligator chose this particular altar," I whispered to Sarah Louise. "Maybe he wanted to be Lozene's handbag. What do you think?"

"Surely you want your children to inherit those jewels?" Peter Earl asked.

"That's one of the tragedies of our lives. We

couldn't have any children, Mr. Jewels. No, those jewels are right there where they belong, with Charlie. He wanted it that way. His other cuff links and tie clips are in there with all the jewels he gave me. I couldn't bear to look at them any longer. See that drawer right up there above his head? Pull it out, Mr. Jewels."

Peter Earl put his hand into the casket and pulled out the drawer, being careful not to touch the top of Charlie's head. The drawer glittered with jewelry, more than I'd ever seen at one time. Dora gasped and Peter Earl grinned.

"It's like King Tut," I whispered to Sarah Louise.

"All he needs is a pyramid," she whispered back.

"Maybe he has one out at the cemetery."

"He must've loved you a whole bunch, Lozene," Dora said. "Don't you think so, Peter Earl?"

He didn't answer. A goofy grin had settled on his face, and his hand was still in the casket. I reached in and pulled it out. Thank goodness Lozene was looking at Dora. "We were so in love, Dora. Thirty-five years of married bliss."

"Did you hear that, Peter Earl?" Dora asked. "Thirty-five years of married bliss."

It was clear to me that Peter Earl hadn't heard anything after seeing all that jewelry. My calling in this church would be simple: keep his hand from the casket and get our show on the road.

"Peter Earl, I'm talking to you," Dora said.

"Pardon, did you say something, Dora?"

Alby Webb walked up and said, "I'd like y'all to meet the funeral director. Come right this way." We followed him out of the sanctuary and into the entryway. A man walked out of the restroom and I jumped. It was Alby Webb's double.

"I'd like you to meet Arnold Webb, director of Webb's Funeral Home. And yes, he is my brother. Twin brother. We each followed our own callings. Arnold was called to death, and I was called to life."

To each his own, I thought, but if I ever got Arnold Webb's calling, I'd pass.

Arnold Webb bowed from the waist and said, "Pleased." His voice sounded like death to me— low, dark, and with a slight whistle. "The funeral will begin in thirty minutes. If you could sit on the front bench with Mrs. Lowdermilk. Watch Alby here, Mr. Jewels, for your cue to arise and proclaim. I believe that Mrs. Lowdermilk wanted you to sing,

Miz Ridley." He turned and led us back into the sanctuary. The front row was empty.

People filed into the church in that coughing, rustley silence of funerals. Alby Webb began the service with the usual "Dearly beloved, we are here to mourn the passing of our dear brother, Charles Eldon Lowdermilk." That was the last thing I heard. My mind was focused on Peter Earl's hands. They kept clenching and unclenching his kneecaps.

Sarah Louise sang, "In the sweet by-and-by, we shall meet on that beautiful shore."

Lozene Lowdermilk collapsed, her sobs separated by long shuddering breaths. How was she gonna make it through the service, poor woman?

Sarah Louise finished the song and sat down. Alby Webb stood up and cleared his throat. "Dearly beloved, we now come to a very important part of our service." He nodded at the soundman in the back of the church.

A scritchy sound came over the PA system, and then a squeaky voice said, "This is Charlie Lowdermilk. I'm speaking to you from the other side." That was the last anyone heard from Charlie Lowdermilk, because Lozene's body lost its starch and she slid down the pew until her knees hit the floor and she pitched forward with a flattening thud. Dora screamed three short bursts and started hyperventilating.

Sarah Louise jumped down on the floor. "Get some smelling salts! Get some smelling salts! Put your head between your knees, Dora, or you will conk out too."

I jumped down beside Sarah Louise and we rolled Lozene over. "Help!" I yelled. "She's cut her forehead and her nose is bleeding!"

"Make way, make way, give me room!" called a woman wearing rolls of black chiffon belted into her rotund middle.

Another woman was close behind her. "Out of my way!" she bellowed. "Miz Emory and I are taking Miz Lozene to the hospital." When they reached Lozene, Sarah Louise and I got up and returned to the front pew.

Peter Earl was looking down into the casket with his back to the pews. How long had he been there? I hoped Charlie Lowdermilk hadn't just parted company with his jewelry.

Alby and Arnold Webb joined Peter Earl in front of the casket. They lowered their heads and whispered for a minute or so. Then Alby said,

"Folks, folks, Miz Moore and Miz Emory are taking Miz Lozene to the hospital. There will be no funeral at this time." Alby and Arnold Webb left. Peter Earl made to follow them out of the church but stopped by the bench where we were sitting and whispered, "I'm going to the hospital with the Webbs. Y'all go on to the motel."

"I'll follow you in my car, Peter Earl," Dora said. "I'm sure Lozene needs me. The girls can walk to the motel."

"No, Dora, you won't follow me," Peter Earl said with unusual stubbornness. "Lozene doesn't need you—she's got plenty of help. Esta Lea needs you." He kissed Dora on the check and whispered something in her ear, and then he ran to catch up with the Webbs.

"I can take care of myself, thank you," I called after Peter Earl.

When the church was almost empty, Dora got up. "Shall we head to the motel? I'm so tired I could—"

"I think I'll walk," Sarah Louise interrupted her. "Y'all go on ahead."

"You? Walk?" I asked. Something funny was going on. Sarah Louise's face was pure rapture as she looked at me and whispered, even though she could have yelled in the empty church, "I owe you big, and I won't forget." Then she left, nearly running.

The Come As You Are Motel was a row of pint-sized cabins about five feet off Highway 22. Dora picked up a key from the manager and unlocked number fourteen. She kicked off her spiked heels, tossed her little pillbox hat onto a chair, and lay down on one of the beds. I lay down on the other one and stared at the ceiling. I tried not to move a muscle so that the sweat beading up on my hairline would not roll down my temples and into my ears.

It grew darker and a blinking neon vacancy sign came on. I wanted to stay awake until Sarah Louise got there, but my eyes kept closing. The slight saw-ing noise coming from Dora's bed must have put me to sleep.

Chapter Fifteen

Treasure

~

For where your treasure is,
there will your heart be also.

Matthew 6:21

A dog was barking somewhere close by, and it woke
me up. I opened my eyes. I was on my side, facing
Dora, who was still wearing her lime green suit. I
rolled over to see if Sarah Louise was awake, but she
wasn't in the bed beside me.

"Dora, Dora! Where is Sarah Louise?"

"What? What?" Dora was shaking her head but
couldn't quite wake up.

I jumped up, grabbed her by the shoulders, and shook her. "Get your brain going, Dora! Sarah Louise isn't here! Her side of the bed wasn't slept in. Where is she?"

"You can stop shaking me now, Esta. I'm awake. Go to the cabin next door and ask Peter Earl. I'm sure he knows something. I didn't talk to him last night on account of I fell asleep. I was so tired, and it must have been late when Peter Earl got back here from the hospital."

I jumped up and ran outside. I banged on Peter Earl's door. "Open up, Peter Earl! We can't find Sarah Louise." I got no answer. "He isn't answering," I yelled back to Dora. Then I looked at the parking lot. Peter Earl's pickup wasn't there.

A gray-haired man stuck his head out of another cabin door and yelled, "Pipe down! Some people are trying to sleep."

Dora came outside. "I'm going down to speak to the manager. I'll get him to unlock the door."

"You better hurry, Dora! Peter Earl's truck ain't here. Come on, we got to get home and tell Mama and Daddy!" I ran back into the cabin and grabbed Dora's purse.

Moments later Dora returned. "The manager

says he never checked in. Now what do you make of that?" she said.

Peter Earl's hand in Charlie Lowdermilk's casket flashed into my mind, but I tried to shake the thought. "I ain't worried about Peter Earl right now. We can find him later. He probably just drove on home. We got to find Sarah Louise."

I remembered my sister's face, and her last words to me, "I owe you for life," settled in. For life. It streaked into my mind then: Jefferson Howard Scott. "We'd better call home," I told Dora.

I phoned from the manager's office. "Mama, Sarah Louise ain't here. We can't find her." That's all I said, because right away Mama told me that Sarah Louise, or Mrs. Jefferson Howard Scott, as she'd become the night before, had just called them.

"I guess I'd better get you home," Dora said.

Dora was quiet on the way home. That surprised me, but there was a first time for everything. She dropped me off and drove away.

Nana was at our house, and Mama was sitting in a chair, crying. "Only seventeen, only seventeen," she moaned.

"It'll be okay, honey. It'll be okay," Daddy said.

He knelt beside Mama, patting her knee and handing her tissues.

"My, my," Nana said, shaking her head. Everyone was repeating themselves.

"But she's a year older than you were, Mama," I said.

"Believe me, it don't help to remind me of that right now," Mama replied.

"Did you know this was gonna happen, Esta Lea?" Daddy asked me.

"No, Daddy, I didn't." I blessed Sarah Louise for keeping this secret to herself. It was the nicest thing she'd ever done for me. I wanted to get Mama and Daddy's mind on something else, so I told them about Lozene Lowdermilk and the service. Neither of them said a word.

"Where's Peter Earl?" Nana said.

"The last time I saw him, he was going to the hospital with the Webbs to see about Lozene. He never checked into the motel last night. He must have stayed with one of the Webbs." I wasn't going to say anything about my suspicions of Peter Earl. They'd had enough bad news for one day. I could tell them tomorrow.

The telephone rang. It was Dora. I listened and then told Mama and Daddy what she said. "Lozene called to tell Dora that the graveside service will be held this morning at ten-thirty. Lozene hoped that someone from our family was still coming. I guess that means me since Peter Earl ain't around and Sarah Louise is on her honeymoon. Dora said I could ride with her to the cemetery because of course she is going. She and Lozene became lifelong friends in the ten minutes before the service started."

"It's the respectful thing to do," Nana said. "Why don't you go along with Dora, Esta Lea."

"I believe Peter Earl must have stayed with the Webbs last night," Dora said when she came to pick me up. "I'm sure he'll be at the service. I just can't figure out why he hasn't called me. Maybe he did and I just missed him in all the running around."

"I don't think so, Dora. I think he got tired of the healing ministry and is moving on to greater things, and I'm betting that Charlie Lowdermilk's jewels will pay for the move. I think that if you was to look in that casket, you wouldn't find any jewels."

"Don't be silly, Esta Lea. Besides, he would have told me."

Somehow I didn't think so. "Why did Lozene put her jewels in the casket anyway? Seems silly to me."

"Love makes people do strange and silly things. Believe me, I know. And to tell you the truth, she's loaded. Those jewels were a drop in the bucket," Dora said. We drove to the cemetery, and Dora turned in under the white grillwork gates.

We walked over to the crowd of people standing around the fresh hole in the ground. It was a much smaller crowd than at the church, but I did recognize Miz Emory and Miz Moore. Peter Earl was not to be seen. Dora lifted up her bangs and dabbed at the sweat on her forehead with a tissue. A pink Caddie pulled up, and Alby Webb got out of it, followed by Lozene Lowdermilk. She had a huge bandage over her nose and a small one on her forehead. Dora knotted her mouth when she saw that Peter Earl was not in the car with them.

Pastor Webb's message began with "Dearly beloved, we are gathered here," and ended with "ashes to ashes, dust to dust." The gravediggers were getting ready to lower Charlie into the ground when Lozene cried, "Stop, stop! I have to say good-bye one last time."

Pastor Alby Webb opened the casket, and Lozene looked in and said, "Oh, my dear little man, good—" And then she started screaming—one of those mad-as-heck screams. "Where in hell is Charlie's diamond tie clip?" She must have said it five times. Then she said, "Open the drawer above his head!" No one moved, so Lozene grabbed Arnold Webb's lapels and said, "You ain't getting one thin dime unless you open that drawer!" He did and everyone gasped.

It was empty.

Lozene jumped up and down. She used her handbag to bang every person standing around the casket. When she got to Arnold Webb, he grabbed her handbag, and it threw Lozene off balance. She tottered, then stepped backward into the open grave. There was a thud and a grunt. The fall had knocked the wind out of her.

I pulled on Dora's arm. "I think this is a good time for us to leave."

Huge gasps were coming up from the grave. Lozene screamed. "My leg, my leg!"

I pulled on Dora's arm again and we went to her car. "Funerals seem to be hazardous to that woman's health," I said as we pulled out of the cemetery.

I didn't say anything to anyone when I got home. I just didn't feel like talking.

When I went to bed that night, my thoughts circled like a dog chasing his own tail. *Where is Peter Earl?* Then, *Where are the jewels?* Then, *Where is the offering money?*

"No more dog-tailed thoughts are bothering me this night," I said finally, and hummed myself to sleep.

Chapter Sixteen

Healing Mercy

Mercy rejoiceth against judgment.

James 2:13

The phone rang. It rang again. And again. I sat up in bed.

"What's going on?" I yelled. When I didn't get an answer, I went downstairs. I poured myself some Lucky Charms cereal and sat down to eat. The morning paper was on the table. Normally I didn't read it, but there was a picture on the front page that caught my eye. It was a woman with her leg in traction. It was Lozene Lowdermilk.

Under her picture was the headline THE HEAL-ING, STEALING JEWELS: WOMAN ACCUSES LOCAL HEALING MINISTRY OF STEALING JEWELS.

The paragraph under this was a quote from Lozene.

"It had to be him, Peter Earl Jewels. The jewels were taken from the casket sometime after the funeral service Sunday evening. Only church folks were around my Charlie, and no one from my church would do a thing like that. They wouldn't dare. And besides, no one has seen hide nor hair of that Peter Earl Jewels since Sunday evening at the church. It's obvious, isn't it?"

There was no doubt in my mind that Peter Earl had stolen those jewels, and now my name would be linked with the "Healing, Stealing" ministry forever. The article ended with the words: "The sheriff is looking for Peter Earl Jewels, the visiting minister. Any news of his whereabouts would be appreciated." I wanted to bust Peter Earl so bad! Stealing the jewels and probably the offerings too! I'd been right about him all along.

My healing calling was finished. Everything was ruined. There would be no more crusades. I wanted to cry, but I was too mad. I pounded the table with my fists until they hurt. If only I hadn't listened to Sarah Louise and waited for one more meeting!

That's when I heard Mama and Daddy. They were on the front porch. The phone started ringing and I answered. It was Nana. "Daddy, it's Nana. She's calling from the hospital."

Daddy and Mama came in, and Daddy took the receiver from my hand. "Oh no," was all he said for a minute or so. "I'll do what I can, but we've had a lot of shocks this morning, Ruby Irene."

"What is it?" Mama asked.

"Uncle Bentley had a heart attack. Ruby Irene went over to his place and found him clutching at his chest. The morning paper was in his other hand. He's in the Good Samaritan Hospital. Ruby Irene asked me to preach at church this Sunday. Esta Lea, you watch Ben while your mama and I go see Uncle Bentley."

It was time for Ben's morning nap. I wished I could nap too, but there wasn't a bit of sleep in me. I read books to him, and it wasn't long before he fell asleep. Thorns were racing up and down my legs, prickling me with energy. I wanted to run and run, but I couldn't leave Ben. I paced the hallway, treading as hard as I could on a loose board in the floor. It seemed like hours before Daddy came home.

His eyes were red rimmed, and the skin on his face seemed to hang in folds. "Your mama is still at the hospital, out in the waiting room. They wouldn't let us stay in there with Uncle Bentley. He isn't doing too well."

"When can I see him?"

"Maybe tomorrow, Esta Lea. I got to work on a sermon. Do you mind watching Ben some more?"

"No, Daddy," I answered. "I'm glad for Ben's company right now."

On Sunday morning my daddy stood behind the pulpit. It reminded me of the last time he was there, about a year ago, when I'd first received my calling. But this time Baby Ben and Adele sat beside me.

Mama and Aunt Phoebe Eileen were back at the hospital with Nana: Uncle Bentley wasn't expected to make it.

"I tried to think of what to preach today," my daddy began, "but nothing came to me. My thoughts were full of Brother Bentley a-laying up there in his bed at Good Samaritan Hospital, and like a light those two words flashed on in my mind— 'Good Samaritan.'

"Now I know it is a familiar story to y'all: A man left home and was beaten up and left for dead in a ditch. A preacher and a churchgoer walked right by him. They figured they'd already done enough good deeds, so they didn't need to help this poor soul. Then along came a man of a despised race. And wouldn't you know it, this despised man was the one who helped the poor soul.

"There is a lot of hurt in this church today, and there is a lot of hurt outside of this church in Beulah Land. Instead of finger pointing and tongue wagging, let's open our eyes and see who needs the love of Jesus. Let's do what Bentley Jewels has done for the last sixty years—let's be Good Samaritans. Let's bring healing to those around us. Most healing comes in bits and pieces, a day and a deed at a time. That's all I got to say."

When Daddy sat down, it was quiet. The quiet went deep inside me. The first time my daddy had preached, God had called me. And now, the second time my daddy preached, God reminded me of that call. There were lots of folks in Beulah Land who needed healing. I'd pray for those around me, and right now that meant Uncle Bentley.

"Adele, can you watch Baby Ben?" I asked. "I got to leave."

"Sure." Adele grabbed Ben and put him on her lap. Willie Boyd was sitting in the back row. I grabbed his arm and pulled him outside.

"Willie, I got to get to Good Samaritan. Can you take me?" I said it before I thought to be shy.

"Why sure, Esta Lea," Willie answered.

I stared out the window on the way to the hospital. *Has to be more pines out there than the sea has waves,* I thought. Every now and then, the glossy leaves of a magnolia poked through the pines. I couldn't let myself think about anything but pines and magnolias.

When we reached the hospital, I opened the

truck door. "Thanks. Don't wait." I decided to take advantage of my new Willie Boyd boldness. I leaned over and kissed him on the cheek. Was he looking at me differently, or was I just imagining it?

The cool dim hallway of the hospital was dizzying after the August heat outside, but the disinfectant smell brought me around real quick.

"Can you tell me where Bentley Jewels is?" I asked Dot, the desk nurse. I knew her from church.

"The waiting room is right down there," she said, "but no one is allowed in with him right now. Not even family. Your mama and your aunt and grandma just left." She turned away at the sound of a buzzer. I looked down on her desk, hoping to catch sight of the room number. I saw 110, BENTLEY JEWELS on a clipboard.

The door creaked when I opened it. Uncle Bentley tilted his head the tiniest bit. Wires and machines crowded his bed. "I'm sorry, Uncle Bentley, I didn't mean to wake you up."

He opened his mouth, but his breath came out in rough patches, so he closed it.

"Don't talk, Uncle Bentley."

He opened his mouth again. He was trying to say something, but his raspy breathing took over.

We both waited. His eyes were determined. Leaning closer, I watched his lips. They seemed to form the words "Peter Earl."

He lifted his pinkie a little, so I reached over to touch it. "Don't try again. Peter Earl is still gone."

A tear slipped out the corner of Uncle Bentley's right eye and rolled down his face. I wiped it away. "I guess he wasn't ready to go on this healing crusade. Maybe you should have tested him at home for a while."

He nodded slightly, so I went on. "Don't worry, Uncle Bentley. I'm still called, anointed, and ordained. I've seen God do mighty things I won't ever forget. But for right now, I'm called to Beulah Land. There is plenty for me to do here."

Uncle Bentley's eyes closed, but his mouth turned up on the left side. I reached over and placed my hand on his chest, wires and all.

"Right here, Jesus!" I prayed. Uncle Bentley jolted and then lay very still. His eyes opened and closed.

"I'm sorry, Esta Lea," he whispered. In a minute his breathing came normal. He even started to snore.

Looks like he's fine now, I thought. That snore is a sure sign. Thank you, Jesus. I watched Uncle

Bentley for a few minutes more. Then I blew him a kiss and tiptoed out of the room.

On the way home from the hospital, I passed Slocum's. The pharmacy was closed on account of it being Sunday, but I could see Patsy inside. She waved at me to come in.

"If it ain't one of the healing, stealing Jewels," Patsy Ann said. "I'm glad you came by. I just tried calling your house, but nobody answered."

"You did? Why?"

"Peter Earl just called me."

"Where is he? What did he say? Did he steal the jewels? Why am I even asking that? I know he did."

"Slow down. Give me a chance. First off, he didn't say where he was or if he stole the jewels. The less we all know, the better. The main reason he called was to leave a message for you. 'Esta Lea had me figured out,' he said. 'Fooled everyone but her, I believe. Tell her the offering is buried underneath the compost pile. I won't be coming home to get it anytime soon.' And then he said, 'Patsy Ann, that girl almost had me converted.'"

"I knew it! I knew Peter Earl stole those offerings! He sure ain't called to the healing business,

Patsy. More likely the money business or monkey business."

Patsy Ann chuckled. "I guess the meetings didn't turn out like you hoped, Esta Lea. But I told you they'd be fun."

I grinned at her. "You were right. But the best part was seeing people get healed and changed."

Patsy went into her office and brought me a Coca-Cola. "For the road, faith healer." It sounded right in spite of everything. "Oh, and say hi to Mrs. Scott for me." News sure got around fast.

"Will do," I promised. The icy pop slid down my throat as I walked home. I pushed the bottle against my forehead to cool me off. As soon as I got in the yard, the screen door banged open and Mama came running out. Daddy was close behind her with Ben in his arms.

"He's healed, Esta Lea, he's healed! Uncle Bentley is healed!" Mama shouted.

"It's a miracle," Daddy said. "I stopped in to see him after church was over, and everyone was shouting and praising. He'd gone from dying to living in a matter of minutes. A miracle! The Lord is good to share him with us for a while longer."

"Get those legs a-pumping! We are going to

praise the Lord!" I said in my best Sister Peggy voice. I saluted toward heaven, whistled, and started marching.

"Amen, Sister!" Daddy shouted.

"Glory, glory!" Mama yelled.

We marched, sang, and shouted around the house. Mama and Daddy headed into the kitchen for some ice tea, but I lingered outside.

I stared up into the heat-shimmering sky and remembered the baptism of fire that I'd received at my calling a year ago. "I hear ya calling me, Lord," I'd said then.

"Keep speaking, Lord," I said now.

ALSO BY CATHRYN CLINTON

Simeon's Fire

Nothing is more important to Simeon Zook than
his family and their farm. But when he's the only
witness to a fire that destroys their barn, Simeon
struggles to tell the truth, especially since he
suspects he's to blame.

"The emphasis is on the love and understanding with
which Simeon's family pulls together, offering a security
that strengthens in times of trial." — *The Horn Book*

"Clinton does a good job translating the simple pleasures
of contemporary Amish life to non-Amish readers."
— *Booklist*

Hardcover ISBN 978-0-7636-2707-2
Paperback ISBN 978-0-7636-3294-6

Available wherever books are sold

Eddie Pittman

AMULET BOOKS
NEW YORK

Library of Congress Control Number: 2015946889

ISBN 978-1-4197-1907-3 (hardback) — ISBN 978-1-4197-1908-0 (paperback)

Copyright © 2016 Eddie Pittman

Book design by Eddie Pittman and Chad W. Beckerman

Published in 2016 by Amulet Books, an imprint of ABRAMS.

Printed and bound in China
10 9 8 7 6 5 4 3

Amulet Books are available at special discounts when purchased in quantity for premiums and promotions as well as fundraising or educational use. Special editions can also be created to specification. For details, contact specialsales@abramsbooks.com or the address below.

ABRAMS The Art of Books
195 Broadway, New York, NY 10007
abramsbooks.com

To Mom and Dad—the storyteller
and the artist, and my first inspirations

Thanks to:

Norm Fuetti, Joshua Pruett, Tom Richmond, Dan Povenmire, Swampy Marsh, Jeff Smith, Kim Roberson, Mike Maihack, Travis Hanson, Tom Dell'Aringa, Steve Ogden, and Broose Johnson for their support, encouragement, and help along the journey.

Travis Hanson, Jose Flores, Sean Balsano, Janelle Bell-Martin, and Ginny Pittman for color and production assistance.

The readers, commenters, and fans of the *Red's Planet* webcomic for keeping me going.

Chad W. Beckerman, Pam Notarantonio, and the whole team at Abrams.

Judy Hansen, my super-ninja agent.

Charlie Kochman, my amazing editor, for taking a chance on this little book.

And to my beautiful wife, Beth, and my amazing kids, Ginny and Teagan—my first and most important audience.

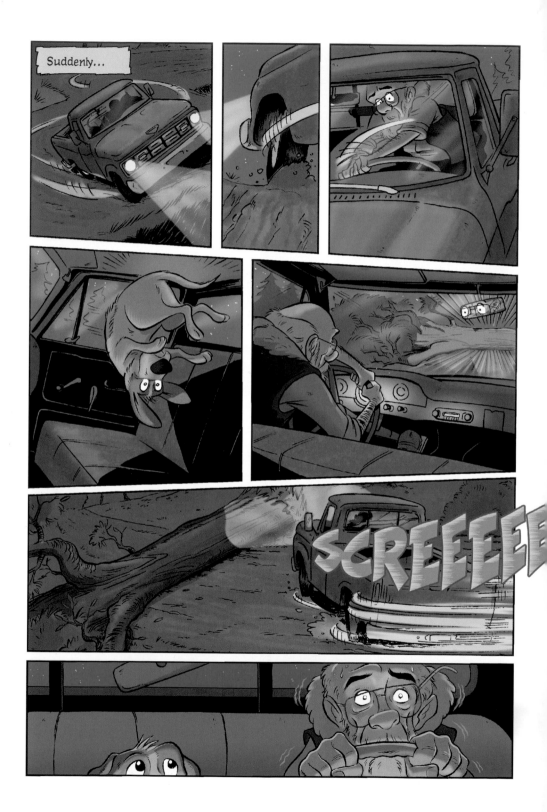

11

14

15

17

18

23

27

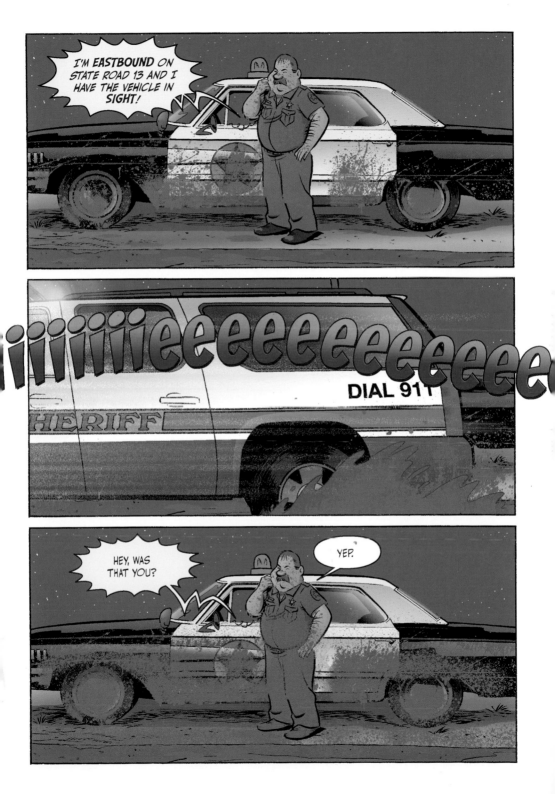

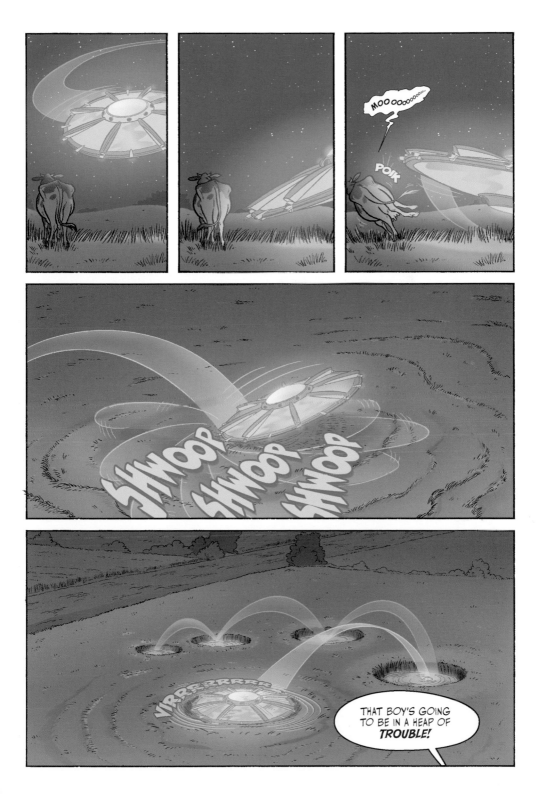

ENGH!

HMPH!

WELL, I THINK THE SHOW'S OVER...

LOOKS LIKE IT'S TAKING OFF.

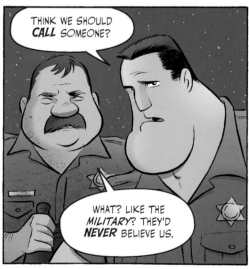

THINK WE SHOULD *CALL* SOMEONE?

WHAT? LIKE THE *MILITARY*? THEY'D *NEVER* BELIEVE US.

YEAH, GUESS YOU'RE RIGHT...

I BETTER GET BACK— GOTTA GET THAT *CAR WASHED* BEFORE THAT *MUD* DRIES!

HEY...I THINK IT'S *COMING BACK!*

37

Chapter Two

More Guests for the Party

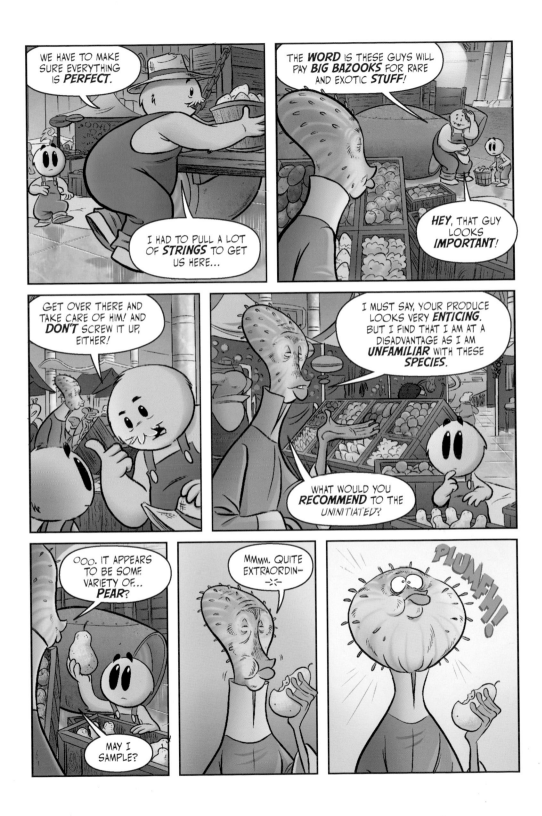

43

48

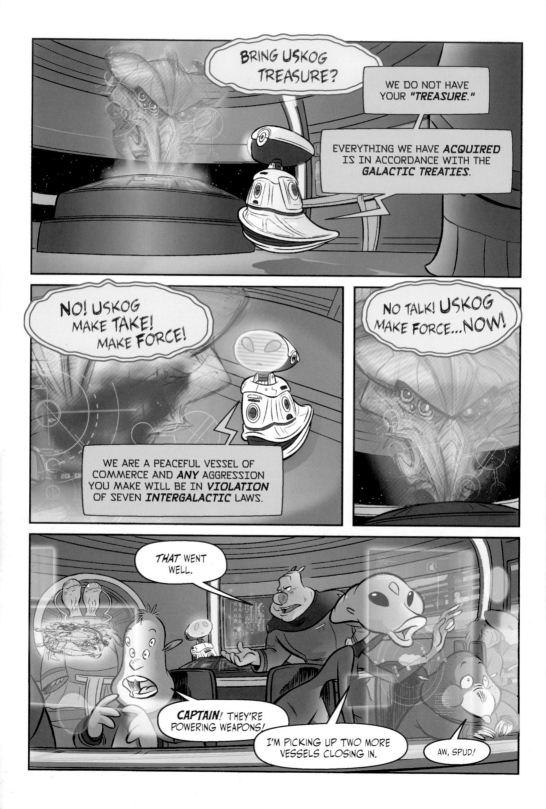

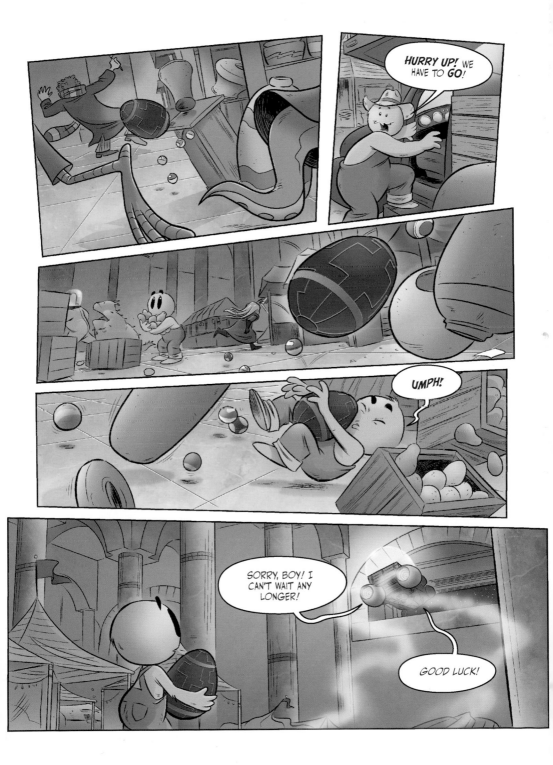

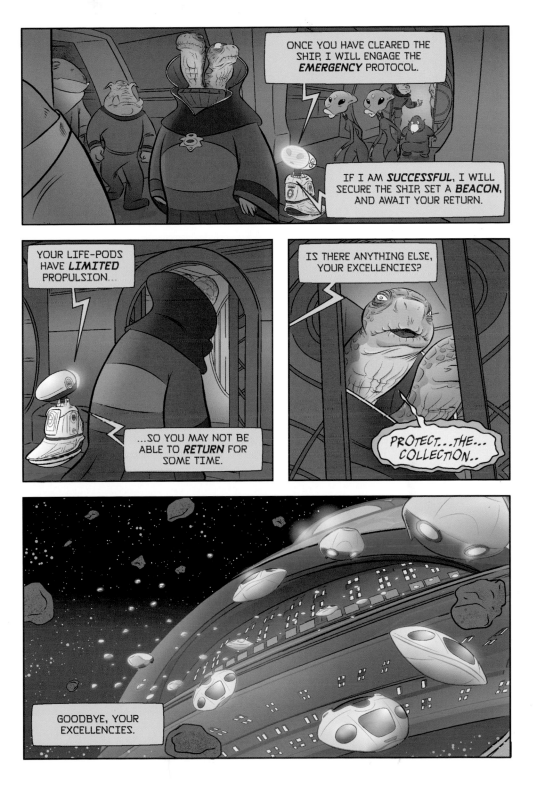

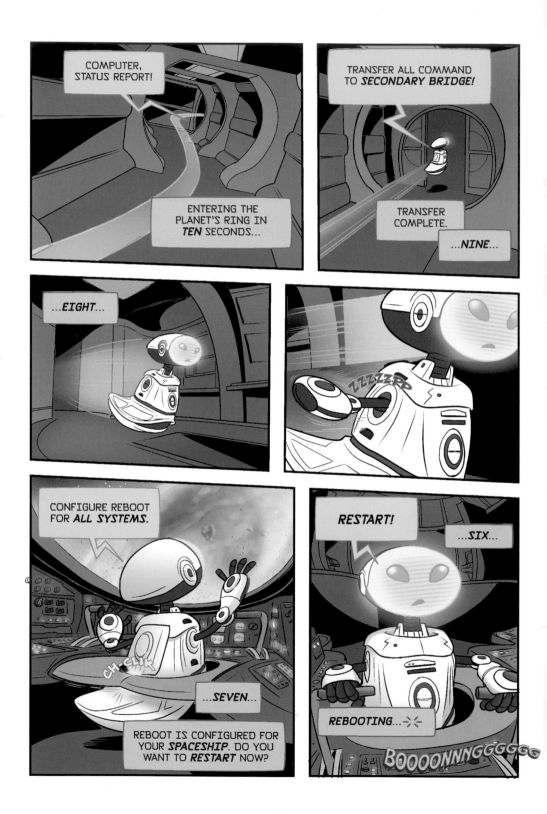

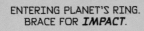

...*ONE*.

ENTERING PLANET'S RING.
BRACE FOR *IMPACT*.

ODDS OF *SURVIVAL*:
SEVEN HUNDRED FIFTY-TWO
THOUSAND TO ONE.

OHHH, THIS *DOESN'T*
LOOK GOOD!

Chapter Three

Aliens are Bad,
Bad People

83

84

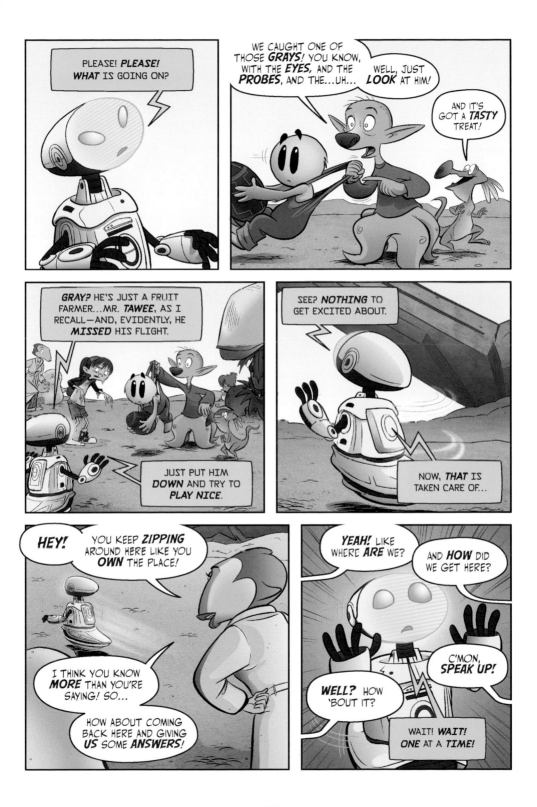

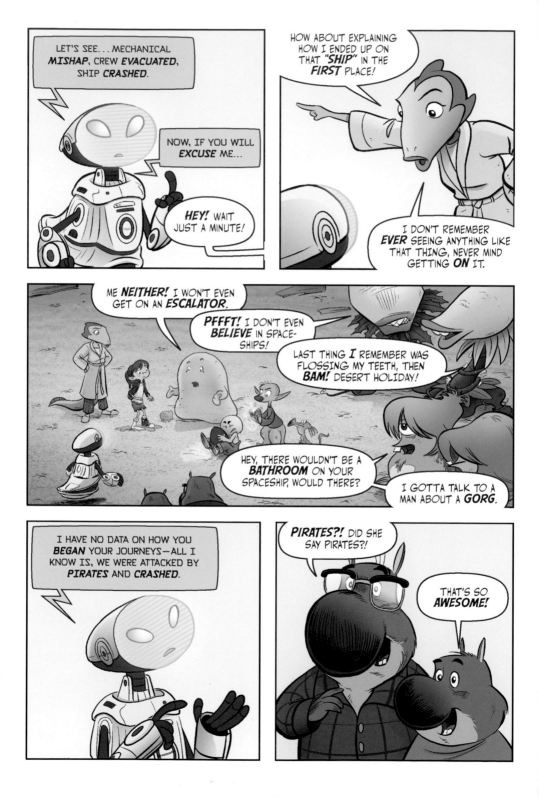

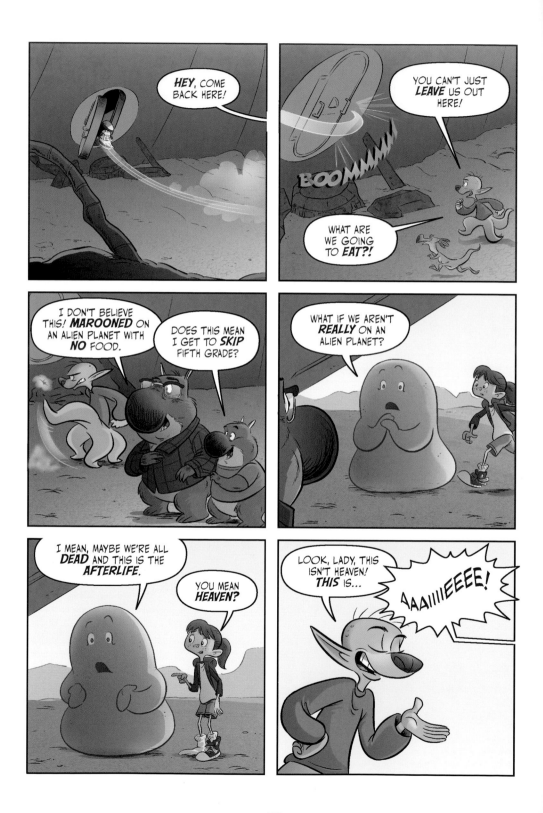

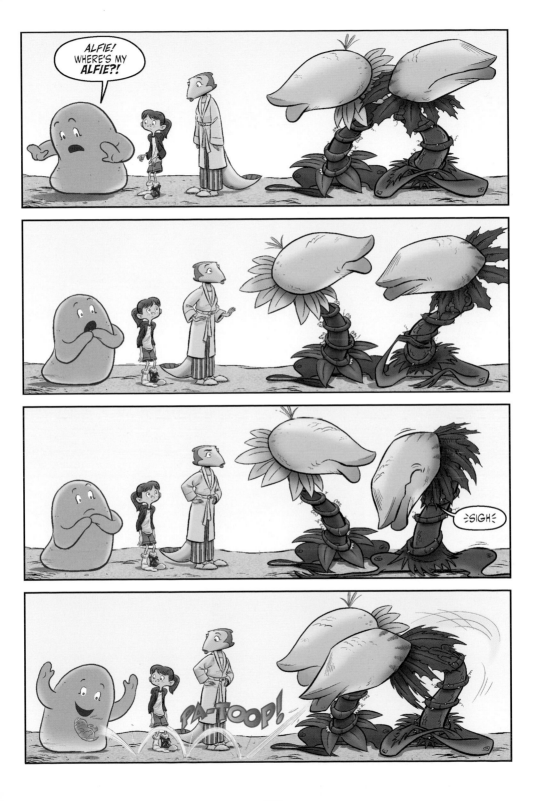

94

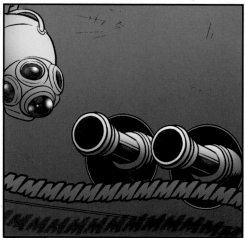

FHUMP

99

102

SO, YOUR NAME IS TAWEE, HUH?

SPLOSSSH

WHA→⤜←

HEY!

WHAT ARE YOU DOING IN THERE!?

117

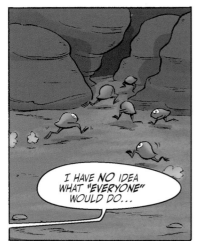

I HAVE *NO* IDEA WHAT *"EVERYONE"* WOULD DO...

BUT I'D START... *RUNNING!*

THAT'S WHAT I *WAS* DOING!

TAWEE?

RUN, TAWEE, *RUN!*

GLIBX

GLIBX

UHHHG.

145

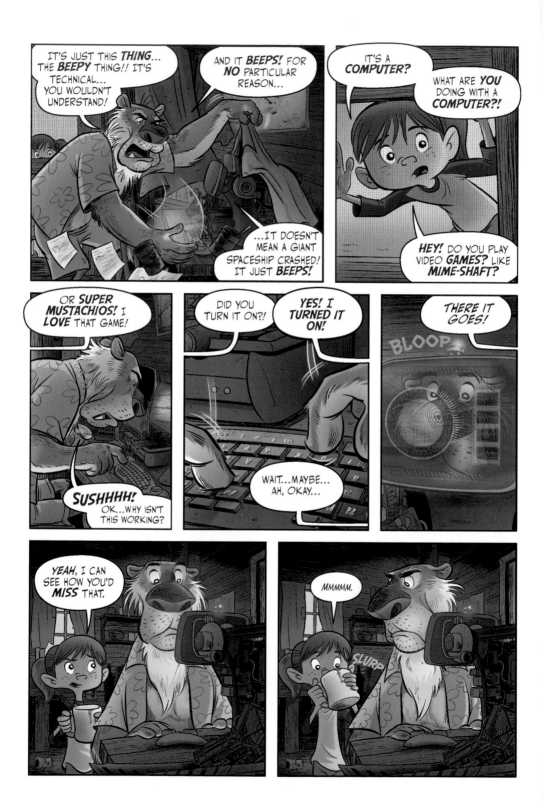

150

WELL, THIS IS CHEERY.

NOT VERY MANY BEINGS FOR A SHIP SO BIG.

WHERE ARE ALL THE OTHERS?

HUH?

IT CAME BACK?

LOVELLE, WAKE UP!

THE *RED ONE*...WITH ALL THE CRAZY *EYES!*

IT CAME BACK! AND IT BROUGHT **SOMETHING** WITH IT!

HEY, LOOK EVERYONE!

IT CAME BACK!

THEY'RE HERE! WE'RE SAVED! ONE MOMENT, PLEASE!

HELLO! I AM *FE*-05251977...

OH!

ARE...ARE... YOU...ALONE?

UH...

WELL...

EXCEPT FOR *THESE* FINE FOLKS, YES. *YES*, I AM.

OH.

OH!

YOU MUST BE THE *FIRST RESPONDER!*

YES! OF COURSE! PLEASE COME IN! *COME IN!*

WOOF!

NOT YOU!

158

159

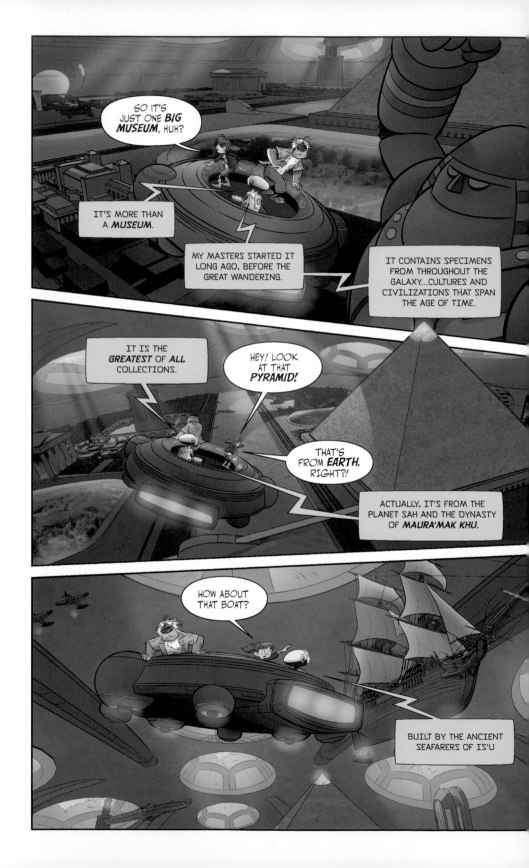

175

177

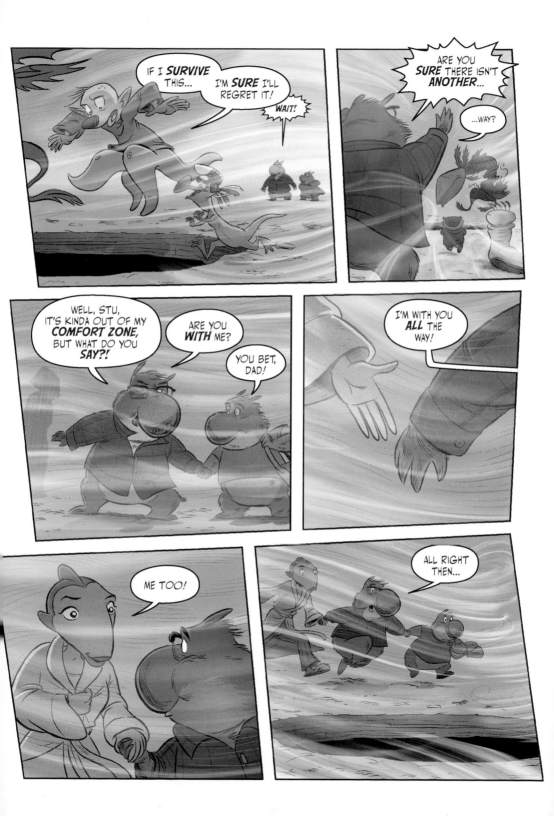

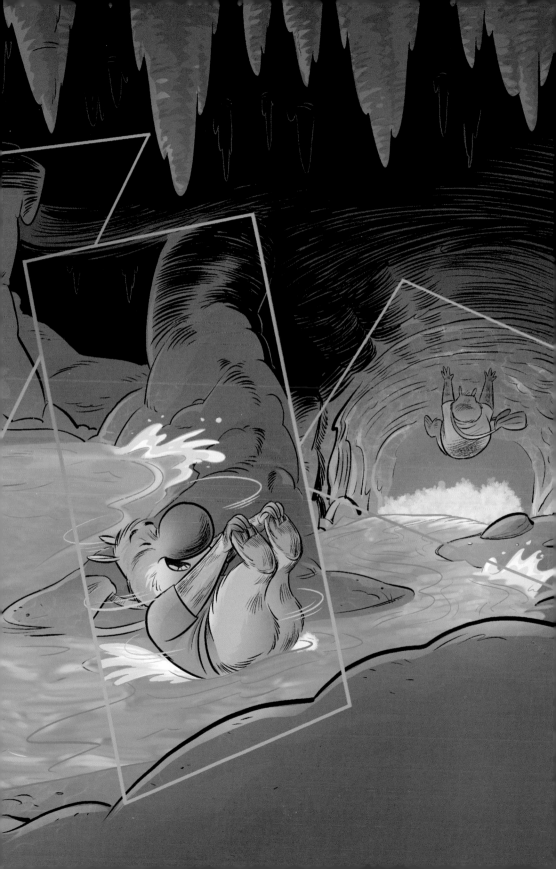

186

THE ADVENTURE CONTINUES IN *RED'S PLANET BOOK TWO: FRIENDS AND FOES*
COMING SPRING 2017